M000158770

THE TRAIL TO RESERVATION

PLAINSMAN WESTERN SERIES BOOK SEVEN

B.N. RUNDELL

WOLFPACK
PUBLISHING
— EST 2013 —

The Trail to Reservation
Paperback Edition
Copyright © 2022 B.N. Rundell

Wolfpack Publishing
5130 S. Fort Apache Rd. 215-380
Las Vegas, NV 89148

wolfpackpublishing.com

Paperback ISBN 978-1-63977-963-5
Large Print Hardcover ISBN 978-1-63977-964-2
eBook ISBN 978-1-63977-962-8

This is dedicated to the memory of so many that paid with blood to open the west and make our great country what it is today. There were those of all races and creeds that carved out their niche in this land, and graves, both marked and unmarked, litter the land. There have been times that I have stood on ground that had been painted with the blood of natives and intruders alike, but our Creator was and is always in control, not as a puppet master, but as the wise master builder He is and always will be, and to that I say Amen! Now, it is up to this generation and those to come to take the raw material they have been given and make it a better place. I pray that they will be up to the task and will be, as long as they trust and depend upon the God of all wonder.

THE TRAIL TO RESERVATION

1 / JOURNEY

The Remington Army .44 caliber pistol hung heavy on his hip, his .52 caliber Sharps rifle lay in the scabbard under his left leg, the stock of the .44 caliber Henry rifle stood high above the pommel of his saddle. The pack mule that followed free-rein close behind his long-legged blue roan gelding, carried the panniers with supplies, a haversack heavy with clothing and other essentials, two parfleches with foodstuffs, and a double-barreled coach gun that lay across the top. Reuben Grundy was a skilled marksman with any weapon, but exceptional with the Sharps. He had spent time in the Berdan's Sharpshooters in the early battles of the civil war, but his wounds gave him an early discharge, although his skills had been put to use by circumstances and the duties of his position as a deputy U.S. marshal for the territory of Colorado. His thick dark blonde hair hung almost to his broad shoulders from under the flat-brimmed black hat. A buckskin jacket with minimal beadwork covered his linen shirt over his dark wool britches tucked into high topped boots.

Riding close beside him was an almost petite and pretty blonde woman whose curls hung past her shoulders and lay atop her fringed buckskin jacket. Elly, Reuben's wife, wore buckskin leggings under a buckskin tunic, attire made for her by their close friends among the Arapaho people. She found the high-topped moccasins more comfortable than the typical footgear for women of the time. Outfitted much like her husband, a Colt Pocket pistol hung on her hip and the stock of her Henry stood above her pommel within easy reach of her right hand. She had become an excellent marksman with both weapons, and skilled with her Flemish knife and metal blade tomahawk. Although it had not been officially recorded, she had also been appointed as a deputy marshal and most often sided her husband in any conflict. The appaloosa mare she rode had been a wedding gift from Red Bear and Running Antelope, women of the Southern Arapaho people.

The sun had spread the gold of early morning across the panorama of the eastern plains as they rode the trail that had become known as the Cherokee Trail, although it had been known by other names in the past. It branched off the Santa Fe trail at Bent's Fort, turned due west before pointing north and on to Denver City and beyond. They were riding into the rising sun, their long shadows stretching behind them, the big black dog they called Bear scouting in the lead. Rolling hills, flat-topped mesas, ragged rock formations, and scraggly piñon offered contrast to the dusty neutral shades of the dry buffalo grass that was pocked with cholla, prickly pear, and occasional hedgehog cactus. The trail rode the southside of the Arkansas River that was marked by a thin line of green as cottonwood, alder, boxelder, and willows that sought the wetlands stretched their branches high for the warm summer sunshine.

The terrain of the plains was deceptive, giving the appearance of vast flat lands, while the low rolling hills, bluffs, and flat-top buttes could hide an entire village of natives, herd of buffalo, and more. With eyes always searching the land around them, both riders were silent, the steady rocking gait of the horses with only the creak of leather and the shuffling of hooves on the dusty trail was mesmerizing. This was the silent time when both Reuben and Elly allowed their quiet thoughts to fill their minds and search for answers to problems and questions.

They had been asked by Governor Evans to go to the plains and do what they could to make the three trails, the Overland, the Cherokee, and the Smoky Hill, safer for the immigration of gold hunters and settlers. They came by stage, wagon, mule train, freighters and even hand carts, but the land they traveled through was contested territory. Although it had originally been the land of Arapaho, Cheyenne, Comanche, and Kiowa, the 1851 treaty of Fort Laramie had made it the land of the Cheyenne and Arapaho. But the renegotiated treaty of Fort Wise of 1861 had reduced the area to a miniscule portion of the original land. Yet it was not just the natives that were resisting the terms of the treaty, but southern sympathizers were robbing stages and freighters under the guise of the war. Further complications were coming from the troops under the command of Major Chivington, the former Methodist preacher, who was in pursuit of a seat in the Senate, thought the only way to have peace was to destroy all natives.

The sun was arching toward its zenith when Reuben nodded toward the riverbank, "Looks like that'd be a

3

good place to noon." Three big gnarly cottonwoods stood tall among the willows, alders, and chokecherry. A slight break in the undergrowth allowed the water of the Arkansas to show itself and bounce diamonds of light about the small clearing as it slowly wound its way to lower climes. As they neared the trees, Reuben stepped down, waited for Elly, and took the leads of both horses and the mule to lead them to water. Elly started gathering some firewood to make a small cookfire for coffee and heating up the leftover biscuits and bacon.

With the animals picketed on the grass, Reuben and Elly found a grey log in the shade of the cottonwood and sat on the ground, leaned back against the log, and sipped the hot coffee. Elly looked at her man and asked, "I can tell by your silence and your expression you've been doing a lot of thinking. What's goin' on?"

He was silent for a few moments, enjoying his coffee and searching his mind for an answer. He began with, "Well, I reckon part of what I'm thinkin' is this marshal thing. When we first agreed with Ben Holladay and the territory marshal to do this, I was thinkin' it was just for the short-time of dealin' with the stage hold-ups and such. Then the governor stepped in and asked for more, and again with this... whatever this is," he rambled, waving his hand around to take in the terrain and their tasks. "Now, don't get me wrong. It's a good thing we been doin', helpin' folks and puttin' outlaws away, cuz somebody's gotta do it. But it's just not what I had in mind for my life," he looked at her and corrected himself, "for *our* life."

He picked up a stick and tossed it toward the simmering coals of the cookfire, glanced at his wife and continued, "When we built our cabin in the Wet Mountain Valley, that's the first time we had anything of our

4

own and it was beginnin' to feel like home. But I also know that nobody will have a home to speak of if there's nothin' but fightin' and killin' and such."

Elly twisted around to lean her arm on the log and look at Reuben, waiting to see if he would say more, and shared her thoughts. "What we've done has been good. But a few good deeds won't totally put evil away. Wherever there are people, there will be both good and bad and if the good people don't stand against the evil, then, well... evil will totally take over and then where will we be?"

Reuben chuckled, looked at his woman and smiled, "At home in our cabin?"

Elly giggled, shaking her head, and said, "On that profound statement, I think we need to get back on the trail." But she did not move, nor did Reuben, whose smile turned into a somber expression.

"Remember when we were with Little Raven and his people?"

"Of course, I'll never forget that. That's when we were married, stayed in the special lodge with his people, and that's when his women gave me Daisy!" nodding toward her appaloosa.

"Yeah, and it's Little Raven's Arapaho and Lean Bear's Cheyenne Dog soldiers that are part of the problem." He paused, turning to face Elly, and continued, "It was his father, Little Owl, who signed the Fort Laramie treaty that agreed the Arapaho and Cheyenne would have all the land between the North Platte River to that," pointing to the water that flowed a few feet away, "the Arkansas River." He pointed to the land on the far side, "All that land from here to the north, and from the mountains to the headwaters of the Smoky Hill River, was to be theirs and white men were to honor that, but

5

they haven't. Settlers and prospectors flooded across the land on their way to the California Gold Rush, and now with the Pikes Peak Gold Rush."

He picked up a small stone and tossed it toward the river, watched it splash and turned back to face Elly. "Now, with the new Fort Wise Treaty, that land has been reduce to a fraction of what it was, but this land," giving a sweeping motion with his arm to indicate the land on the north side of the river, "is still theirs. But that hasn't kept the settlers out."

Elly nodded, frowned, "Didn't Little Raven say he and Chief Niwot make peace with the gold seekers?"

"He did, and he has always been for peace. But if you remember, when we met him, he and his people were further north on a buffalo hunt. He admitted that was off the land that was supposed to be their reservation, but they had not been given the rations promised and his people were hungry. So, they went on a buffalo hunt."

"He said he thought war would come between the Arapaho and the whites," mused Elly, slowly shaking her head.

"And I'm thinkin' war is here. It's not just the Arapaho, it's also the Cheyenne, especially the Dog Soldiers of Lean Bear, and there's some Lakota and Kiowa also involved."

"So, are we supposed to keep peace with all those? What about the outlaws and rebels that are hitting the stages and freighters?"

Reuben shook his head, tossed another rock, glanced at his woman, and said, "Complicated, ain't it?"

"Ummhmm. But I think that calls for a short nap!" declared Elly, scooting down into the grass beside the log, and slipping her hat over her eyes as she crossed her arms over her chest, crossed her legs at her ankles, and mumbled, "You could use one too!"

Reuben chuckled, motioned to Bear to come near, and said to the big dog, "You keep watch for us boy, we're gonna get a little shuteye."

2 / STAGE

The bright afternoon sun pierced the spotty shade from the cottonwoods and pried open the eyelids of Reuben. The warmth felt good, but time was slipping by, and they needed to be on the trail down the Arkansas valley. He rolled over to look at Elly who was sleeping but with a broad smile on her face and he chuckled as he reached to touch her face. "Hey sleepyhead, we need to get a move on!"

She slowly came awake, knowing the voice of her husband also assured safety and security. She rolled to the side, still smiling, and looked at her man, "I was dreaming."

Reuben chuckled, "And just what were you dreaming that put such a smile on your face?"

She giggled, jumped to her feet, and gave a coy smile as she answered, "That's for me to know and you to find out!" Trotting to the horses with a glance over her shoulder, she snatched up the lead of her appaloosa and pulled her close to start tightening the girth to be ready to leave. As Reuben came beside her, the lead of the blue roan in hand, she asked, "So, are we going to the fort or to Bent's ranch?" She knew his plan was to find William Bent and talk to him about the troubles with the natives and to see if he had any information about the stage robberies.

"Wherever we can find Bent, I reckon."

It was pushing close to mid-afternoon and the trail had shown little more than an abundance of long-eared snowshoe rabbits often chased by hungry coyotes as they zigzagged in and out among the sage, greasewood, and rabbit brush. Reuben and Elly were side by side, Bear well out in front on his scout of the trail, when beyond the rise in the hills before them came the distant sound of rumbling thunder. They looked at one another, frowning, and scanned the sky that was totally devoid of any clouds. Reuben turned to face Elly as he stated, "Gunfire!"

Elly nodded as they reined up and looked at her man, "But from what?"

"This is a stage road," pointing the trail with his chin, "and I'm guessin' the stage is getting attacked, either by Indians or outlaws. He pointed just off the trail to a rock formation, "You take that! I'll take the brush yonder. When the stage nears and we can see what's chasin' 'em, then..." and shrugged, leaving the choice up to her.

With a quick nod, she dug her heels into the ribs of Daisy and made for the stack of rocks. Before the appaloosa slid to a stop, Elly was swinging out of the saddle, rifle in hand. She grabbed the reins, led the mare to a slight overhang of the rocks to put her out of sight of the trail, then quickly mounted the rocks and dropped behind a boulder that stood atop the slight rise. She looked at the trail, then across the road to see where Reuben had positioned himself. He was moving through the brush, saw her and waved, then ducked out of sight behind a thick cluster of sage.

They were no sooner in position, when the gunfire and screaming foretold the appearance of the stage as it crested the slight rise between the flat-top buttes. They heard the big bark of the coach gun as the messenger or shotgunner tried his best to discourage the attackers. The Jehu or driver was cracking his long bull whip that sounded like a pistol shot, urging the six-up of lop-eared mules to quicken their step. A billowy cloud of dust rose behind them, masking the attackers.

But the screamed war-cries told Reuben and Elly all they needed to know, this was an attack by Indians and as Reuben thought about it, he guessed they were Dog Soldiers of the Cheyenne or the Kiowa. The Dog Soldiers were a militant arm of the Cheyenne who had refused to honor the treaty signed by several of the tribe's head men, declaring the treaty to be invalid because it had not been presented to the council of forty leaders nor the people of the Cheyenne nation. Several of the attackers were firing pistols, but most were using the traditional bow and arrow.

As they neared, Reuben saw the shotgunner frantically reloading his coach gun and the driver shouting to his team. The attackers were gaining ground and would soon overtake the coach. A quick glance showed at least one passenger trying to shoot from the window of the coach, but none of their efforts were showing results.

The coach was just about a hundred yards away when Reuben opened fire. His first round unseated a warrior, and as he jacked another round into the chamber, he heard the sharp report of Elly's Henry. As he picked another target, he saw one of the warriors, slump forward on his horse, having taken a slug from Elly's rifle. He swung the muzzle away, chose another rider and fired.

The coach was rocking on its thoroughbraces, trace chains rattling, mules grunting, and lathering up, feet digging into the dirt of the trail and the coach gun of the shotgunner barked again and again. Reuben and Elly had laid down a deadly barrage, easily dropping six or more riders, and as the coach drew near, the screaming of war cries lessened, and the leaders had shouted their orders as the remaining five or six warriors turned away and disappeared in the big dust cloud.

Neither Reuben nor Elly moved, but kept their position, watching the dust cloud dissipate and the warriors ride over the crest of the rise. They had lost about half their number in an attack they had presumed would be an easy victory that would gain them additional weapons and plunder, but they knew the cost was too high and would probably not return. As the dust settled, Reuben rose from the brush, looked toward the rock formation, and waved, prompting Elly to stand up and wave back. They went to their horses and mounted up, swinging toward the stage that had stopped a couple hundred yards down the road.

The cottonwoods had grown thick along the riverbank and the driver was nudging his mules toward the river. They had worked hard and would need a long drink and a short rest. The shotgunner stood beside the four passengers and watched as the two riders approached. He stepped behind the coach, big shotgun in hand and watched as they came near. He grinned wide enough to show his tobacco-stained teeth, even from the distance of thirty yards as he hollered, "Boy, I was never so glad to hear your shootin'! You saved our skins!" He pushed off his hat and rubbed his bald head, "I weren't too worried 'bout muh scalp, since I ain't got none, but I seen what them Kiowa can do to a fella and I don't mind tellin' ya, I was skeered!"

Reuben and Elly drew close, Reuben leaned on his pommel with crossed arms and said, "You sure they were Kiowa?"

"Youbetcha! Them fellers have that roach at the back of their heads, feathers all a flutter, an' many of 'em have that hairpipe breastplate. They're easy to spot by that big roach at the back of their head, though, ain't no others use that!" declared the shotgunner. He looked from Reuben to Elly and frowned, "Hey! You're a woman!" His remark drew the attention of the four passengers that were following the coach to the water but turned at the declaration, shading their eyes to look.

Elly laughed, "You don't say! I was kinda thinkin' the same thing!"

The shotgunner began sputtering and fussing, shaking his head and grinning, "I just dint 'spect no woman to save my bacon from a bunch a screamin' Kiowa!"

Bear had dropped to his belly between the horses and sat with tongue lolling out as he looked at the shotgunner, a diminutive man with a pot belly, sagging britches that stretched his galluses, a weathered and worn buckskin jacket that was missing most of its fringe, and high-topped boots that reached to his bow-legged knees. The man sat the coach gun's butt on the toe of his boot, crossed his arms atop the muzzle and grinned, shaking his head and muttered, "I'll just shut up now 'fore I get muhself in real trouble!"

Reuben led the way to the river to give their horses a drink. The driver had unhitched the team and led them to the water, giving the big mules a long and well-deserved drink. He was leading them away from the water when Reuben stepped down from Blue, nodded at the man and started to the water.

"You the one's what run them red-devils off?" asked the Jehu.

"You might say that, but that coach gun was barkin' pretty loud, too," answered Reuben.

"Hummph, that's about all those things are good for is makin' a big noise. They ain't no good at any distance, but Baldy does his best, I reckon." He paused, looking from Reuben to Elly and asked, "You folks do that often? I mean, jumpin' into fights you didn't pick?"

"Just doin' our best to help out, that's all," answered Elly, walking past the man and leading Daisy to the water. She shook her head and walked on, leaving the talking to her man.

"Didn't mean no disrespect. I'm mighty grateful for what you done. It's just that there's a lot o' folks would just find a hidey hole and wait till it was all over, but you didn't, and thanks for that!"

Elly waved over her shoulder and led Daisy out on the sand bar for her drink. She glanced back and saw Reuben was still talking to the man and watching the passengers belly down and get a drink of the cool clear water of the Arkansas River. She shook her head and muttered, "Pilgrims!"

The mules had walked across the sandbar and out into the water before getting their fill and returning to the bank. The Jehu quickly re-hooked the trace chains and lined out the teams, stretching the ribbons or reins up into the box to wrap around the break lever. The mules stood quiet, occasionally stomping a foot, swishing a tail, or shaking a head, anything to show their impatience about getting back on the road. Reuben and

Elly swung back aboard, and with a hand motion to Bear, sent him on his scout, and Reuben grabbed up the lead for the mule and with a wave to the men, started back on the trail, hopeful of making up for the lost time and finding a good camp for the night. It would be another day before they made it to either Bent's ranch or Fort Lyon.

3 / BENT

"That's right, this shipment is all for a C.W. Kitchen and Buckskin, we are headed there now. But, señor, I haf never been to Buckskin, but I'm told I can follow the Arkansas to Cañon City an' from there up to Fairplay and on to Buckskin," explained Jose Padilla, the captain of the freighters bound for South Park. They had come from Westport, Missouri under contract with C. W. Kitchen and his mercantile store in Buckskin.

Reuben grinned, "So this is your first trip to Buckskin?"

"Si, señor, but not my first trip to this country," waving his hand about him, taking in the valley of the Arkansas. "What can you tell me about the trail?"

"If'n I was you, I'd swing north out of Pueblo, cut west to Colorado City, and on into South Park. The road through that country is better traveled, and much easier than anything out of Canon City, and it's not any further and it is better road."

"Si, si. I have heard of this Colorado City. Perhaps we will go that way."

"Then maybe you can help me. I haven't been

15

through this country, and we're bound for Fort Lyon and Bent's ranch. We're lookin' for William Bent."

"Ah, si! It is not far. The ranch of Bent is on the Purgatoire River, south of the confluence with the Arkansas. It is easy to find, the land it is flat and there are few ranches. Fort Lyon is further, maybe ten miles or so, and on the north of the Arkansas."

"That's what we were told before. Have you had any trouble with the Indians?"

"No, senor. We saw some near Fort Lyon, but they did not come near. We have too many men, all well-armed." He nodded toward the group of men that were mostly gathered near the cookfire, awaiting the evening meal. Reuben had already noticed the four men stationed on guard and guessed there to be about fifteen to twenty men for the six big freighter wagons. Each of the wagons had a four-up team of big mules and there were about twenty or more horses in their remuda. Although it would be a tempting target for the natives, it was also a prohibitive risk for the natives who would usually move in war parties of about twenty warriors and to go against a band of men, all armed with modern rifles, Spencers, Springfields, and Sharps, could be costly for the attackers.

"There was a band of Kiowa that attacked a stage yesterday, about ten miles west of here, so you might keep a sharp eye out, although they lost a handful of their warriors and might not be too anxious to try it again," explained Reuben, lifting his coffee cup to his lips. He tossed the dregs of the coffee aside, sat the cup upside down on the rock and rose to his feet. "Reckon we'll be turnin' in. I s'pose you men'll be leavin' early in the mornin'?"

"'Fore first light!" declared Jose, nodding, and finishing his cup of coffee.

"Since we're goin' in opposite directions, you men have a good 'un," suggested Reuben.

"Si, si. And vaya con Dios!"

"And you as well," replied Reuben, turning from the fire to go to their camp that was set apart from the freighters in the edge of the trees near the river.

———

Mid-morning saw Reuben and Elly approaching the confluence of the Purgatoire and Arkansas Rivers. The cottonwoods stood tall along the Arkansas, but the smaller Purgatoire that came from the south, held mostly scattered willows, alders and serviceberry, current and chokecherry bushes. The shallow river held many marshes thick with cattails and bluestem and sedge grasses. As they neared the river, Reuben reined up, stood in his stirrups, and looked around, searching for a trail or road that might lead to the ranch of William Bent. He shaded his eyes and looked to the south to see the silhouette of a flat-top adobe structure that stood slightly above a stockade. He grinned, nodded toward the sight, "That looks like it! From what the freighters said, that's gotta be Bent's ranch. Now, if only he's to home!" He dropped into his saddle and reined Blue toward the dim trail that followed the west bank of the Purgatoire and pointed toward the stockade.

Elly stayed at his side, "And if he's not there?"

Reuben huffed, "Dunno. We were told he'd be the best source of information 'bout what's happenin' around these parts, both with the natives and pilgrims. So, I'm hopin' he'll be there and be willing to talk to us."

As they neared the stockade which was neither large nor imposing in comparison to the Big Timbers Fort that had been built by this same man, but it was sufficient for protection and defense for a small group, they slowed their approach, taking in everything. Although William Bent had built his first trading fort twenty years prior, and the second newer fort called Big Timbers, less than a decade past, that fort had been leased to the Army and was currently being used for storage of the rations and more for the Cheyenne and Arapaho that were reservation bound. With this being Bent's home, and that he had been friends with the many different natives, he had little to fear from any of the tribes. Three hide lodges were standing to the west of the stockade, thin tendrils of smoke rising from cookfires tended by women in native dress.

The big gate was open, and they rode inside, looking around cautiously but focused on the long-covered porch of the main house, where a man sat in a rocking chair and watching the newcomers. He lifted a hand, "Mornin'! Step down if you're friendly." He was puffing on a pipe and the smoke rose above his partially bald head.

"Mornin'," answered Reuben. "I'm Reuben Grundy and this is my wife, Elly. If you don't mind, we'd like to talk to you a spell."

"Certainly. And I'm William Bent. Join me!" he answered as he waved his pipe toward a pair of ladder-back chairs and a bench.

Reuben stepped down, reached up to assist Elly as she swung a leg over the rump of the appaloosa and leaned back into his arms. He easily lowered her to the ground, nodding to the porch and as she stepped away, he loosened the girth on the appy, stepped around Blue

18

and loosened his girth. With the horses and mule tethered at the hitchrail, Reuben followed Elly up the three steps to the porch. Reuben extended his hand to Bent, "Mr. Bent, pleased to meet'chu."

Bent accepted his hand, shook it as he looked up to Reuben, then motioned to the chair for him to be seated beside Elly. "So, what brings the two of you to my home?"

Reuben leaned forward, his elbows on his knees as he began, "Well sir, the governor asked us to come."

Bent frowned, leaning forward, and spat, "The governor sent you to see me?"

"Not to see you, but to do what we could to, well, to stop the stage hold-ups and such."

Bent fumed, shaking his head, "That sounds like that worthless whelp! Five different tribes of native people up in arms because he and his political cohorts can't keep a treaty! Raids goin' on and people gettin' killed, cuz they ain't gettin' their annuity goods and are starvin', and he sends *two* people, and one a woman, and thinks it'll put a stop to it! No wonder he wants to be a senator! He wants to go to Washington and get rich with all the other crooks!" He huffed around, looking about his compound, and shaking his head, then looked back at Reuben, "And you fell for it? You got a death wish or somethin'?"

Reuben chuckled, shaking his head as he sat back and looked at Bent. "No, but we've had a little success with things and if we can do anything that'll help, then we'll give it a try."

Bent frowned, shaking his head as many thoughts and memories flitted through his mind of others that thought they could do something and were now nothing but memories, both good and bad, as their bones

19

bleached in the hot sun of the great plains. He looked at Reuben, "Tell me about yourselves and what makes a man bring his wife into this, this..." he mumbled as he waved his hand to take in his surroundings. He sat back in his chair, puffed on his pipe, and looked at Reuben, waiting for an answer.

After a short pause to gather his thoughts, Reuben began, "First off, you need to understand we did not ask for this," waving his hand as did Bent, "but I reckon it all started with Ben Holladay..." and he began to relate many of the happenings of the past couple years from his coming west, meeting Elly, getting appointed marshals, and helping the Overland Stage Company. He ended with their recent incursions with the Reynolds gang and getting the telegram from the governor about the problems on the Cherokee, Smoky Hill, and Overland trails.

"Well, you have been busy, I'll give you that. But what do you know about the natives, you know, the Arapaho, Cheyenne, Lakota, Kiowa, Comanche and such?" queried Bent.

Reuben glanced to Elly and back to Bent, "Can't say much about the Lakota, but we're friends with Little Raven and his Arapaho," he paused as he saw the brow of Bent wrinkle as his long eyebrows shaded his thin piercing eyes that showed disbelief. But Reuben continued, "did a little trading with Lean Bear and the Cheyenne Dog Soldiers, were neighbors with the Mouache Ute and the Jicarilla Apache, fought the Comanche and just recently had a little set-to with some Kiowa. Didn't talk much though."

"Hold on. You're friends with Little Raven?"

"That's right, spent some time with him and his family."

Bent frowned, his eyes narrowing even more, "And you traded with Lean Bear?"

"Ummhmm."

"Lean Bear's dead. Got killed by a wet-behind-the-ears lieutenant name of Eayer. Lean Bear rode out to parley with the sojer boy and was shot down. The lieutenant turned tail and run back to Fort Larned. Happened this spring," he stated, dropping his eyes to the floor, shaking his head. He looked up at Reuben, "What kinda tradin' did you do with Lean Bear?"

Reuben grinned, "He had a couple white women captives and we traded him a Sharps rifle for the both of 'em."

Bent let a slow smile split his face, looking from Reuben to Elly, "Seems to me I heard about some woman gettin' the better of that ol' chief!" He chuckled, looked to Elly, "Was that you what done it?"

Elly smiled, slowly nodded, "Yessir, it was. But it was all in good fun. We were determined to get the women back, one way or another."

Bent looked back to Reuben, grinning, "And how do you know Little Raven?"

Reuben glanced to Elly again, smiling, "Little Raven did the joining ceremony for us to get married. He had a marriage tipi set up and we stayed the week with his family. His wife gave Elly that appaloosa there," nodding toward Elly's mare.

"Well…you just might be able to help things out after all," answered Bent. He slowly stood, stepped to the edge of the porch and knocked the dottle from his pipe, turned and said, "My wife, Yellow Woman, took my son Charley, and left to return to her people. But my wife, Island is out yonder by the lodges, and she's been fixin' a

21

meal for us. So, how's 'bout the two of you joinin' us for a meal?"

"That would be fine," answered Reuben, standing. He looked to the horses, "Should we leave them here?"

"That'll be fine. We'll eat, talk a little, then decide what we'll be doin' next," answered Bent, taking to the steps to lead the way to the lodges.

4 / PARLEY

They sat cross-legged, carved wooden trenchers or platters on their laps, but talked little during the mid-day feast. Although it was a tranquil scene, two other women helped Island, Bent's third wife, as she prepared and served the meal, and the location of the lodges atop a slight knoll beside the stockade offered a view of the bosque of the Purgatoire River as it made its way to the confluence with the Arkansas. The sky was clear, the blue canopy giving its usual backdrop to the vast expanses of the great plains that stretched beyond the extent of their vision, and the bright sun warmed their backs. Elly looked at Reuben, her fingers cupped to hold a mouthful of stew, "What kind of meat is this? It's tender and tasty, but different. Is it antelope?"

Reuben chuckled, looked around and noticed Bear lying beside Elly, leaning closely against her. With a grin he said, "Have you noticed there are no dogs around?"

Elly's face melted into a somber expression, eyes wide as she slowly looked around the camp and back to Reuben as she whispered, "You don't mean..." she asked as she unconsciously reached down to pull Bear closer.

Reuben chuckled, slowly nodding his head as he took another bite of the stew. "And if you don't eat, it will be an insult to the women," he nodded in the direction of the native women.

Elly looked toward the women, down at her food and up at Reuben, "But..." she frowned and held the plate away as her nose wrinkled and the frown painted her face in despair.

Reuben chuckled, "At least try to look like you're eating," he whispered.

———

BEYOND THEIR LITTLE CLUTCH, AND NEARER THE FARTHEST hide lodge, a white-haired man sat leaning on a willow back rest, a trencher on his lap as he was tended to by another woman. Two youngsters sat beside the old man, quietly focused on their own plates. Bent saw them looking at the man and spoke softly, "That's White Thunder. He was a great chief of the Cheyenne and the father of my women. He arranged my first marriage with Owl Woman, and as is the custom of the people, I later took her sisters, Yellow Woman, and Island," nodding to the woman that had prepared and served their meal, "as my wives. Owl Woman died in the cholera epidemic, but Yellow Woman took care of our children. She left with Charley, *Pe-ki-ree,* meaning White Hat, our son, and he joined the Dog Soldiers. Now my other son, George, *Ho-my-ike,* has joined them and lives with the Cheyenne." He looked down, shook his head and looked back, "And that's after he went to school and college back east. But he likes the life with the Cheyenne, and I understand that."

"Did you have any daughters?" asked Elly, doing her

best to keep down the meat without gagging as she chewed.

"My oldest was Mary, *Ho-ka,* and she is with the Cheyenne, and youngest was Julia, *Um-ah,* and she married Edmund Guerrier, a trader and rancher who is also part Cheyenne." He sat his trencher aside, reached for his coffee cup and leaned back against the willow back rest and took a long sip. "So, if you're gonna be doin' whatever you can for peace, maybe I should tell you a little about the people and the problems."

Reuben nodded, also setting his plate aside and picking up the coffee cup. Leaning back, he turned slightly to face Bent and nodded, "That would be very helpful." He glanced to Elly who had copied the men and sat back, ready to listen and learn.

"I've been here for, oh, goin' on thirty-five years. And from the beginnin', I've dealt with every tribe of natives that have been in this land," he waved his hand to take in all the terrain in a grand swoop, "But the Cheyenne have always been special. My wives were Cheyenne and I've lived with them and the Arapaho, as well as the Kiowa, Comanche, Sioux and others that have traded with us at the forts, and we've been friends with them all, some better'n others."

He took a long sip of coffee and continued. "But this year, things have gotten worse. I reckon it's because of all the gold hunters and settlers coming through and payin' no heed to the natives, 'ceptin' maybe to kill 'em, and that of course caused the natives to seek a little retribution." He paused again, "I reckon the biggest problem is the whites just don't understand the natives, their way of life, and such. They don't live nor think like the white man."

"Like early this summer, up north a spell, a band of

raiders, prob'ly Arapaho with Notnee or Roman Nose, hit a ranch and killed the family of one of the ranch hands, a fella by the name of Hungate. Now, I don't know exactly what happened, but because it was a bloody mess, the folks in Denver called it the Hungate Massacre and got all upset, understandably." He nodded and took another drink, "But nobody was upset when Major Downing went against the Cheyenne and killed twenty-five and wounded forty, or when Lieutenant Eayer faced off with Lean Bear who wanted to parley, and the wet-behind-the-ears officer shot him down without a word bein' said! And if it wasn't for Black Kettle stopping them, the dog soldiers would have followed them killers back to Fort Larned and wiped them out!" He shook his head and squirmed around trying to stifle his anger and get comfortable.

He glared at Reuben, took a deep breath and continued, "Sorry, that kinda gets muh dander up. So, after that I went to see Black Kettle. But that was after I learned from Major Wynkoop, who, by the way, is 'bout the only sojer boy I've met that has any sense when it comes to the natives, that Chivington and Evans have decided the only way to deal with the natives is to kill them all, thinking that's the only way to have any peace at all!" He paused again, "So, when I was talkin' with Black Kettle, he wanted me to know that he and the Southern Cheyenne, most of 'em anyway, planned on stayin' outta the war that the Dog Solders and Sioux declared on the whites! So, I said I'd do what I could to talk to General Curtis and try for peace. But when I got back to Fort Lyon, Chivington was there and said that I had no right to request a parley with Black Kettle, and that Curtis had ordered all Colorado troops to attack all Indians! He also said he was personally 'on the warpath' and wasn't gonna stop till all Indians are kilt!"

He leaned back again, shaking his head and tossed the dregs of his coffee to the side, motioning to Island to pour him some hot coffee. As she filled his cup, he continued, "That was when that Indian agent Colley said that Evans wanted some kinda peace that would keep the friendly Indians from getting killed, and that he was sending Chivington back with some money to provide for the rations and such for the friendlies."

He sipped again, "So, I went back and talked to some of the chiefs of the different tribes and several of 'em came with me to Fort Larned, and we found Captain Parmetar sober and got a tentative truce, and they promised more annuities and trade goods to the peaceful tribes. Now, that was just last month." He breathed heavy, leaned forward and added, "Since then some o' the Dog Soldiers and Sioux have been raidin' up north on the Overland Trail and Smoky Hill."

He chuckled as he remembered, and with a smile of mischief looked up at Reuben, "Then the Kiowa chief, Satanta, goes to Fort Larned and asks for a parley with Parmetar. Now, Satanta had him some 'firewater' and some pretty squaws and so Parmetar and some o' his men went on a bender with Satanta. But when they woke up, Satanta and his men had killed a sentry an' stole o'er two hundred horses and mules, him and the squaws made a clean getaway! And ol' Parmetar was mad, whoooeee, he was mad!" chuckled Bent, laughing at the thought.

He sobered quickly and looked sternly at Reuben, "Then the Arapaho chief Left Hand approached the fort with a white flag, wanting a parley. He was gonna tell Parmetar where he could find the stolen horses, but

Parmetar was still mad and fired a howitzer at Left Hand's party. So, that chief high-tailed it and ain't interested in any peace with them sojer boys!" He laughed again, "And now they've closed the Overland Trail and will prob'ly be closin' the Smoky Hill trail!"

As he sat shaking his head and occasionally sipping his hot coffee, he glanced up at Reuben and Elly, "So the way I see it, the natives, just 'bout all of 'em, have tried to make peace, but the soldiers with their drunken officers and those bent on killin' em all, just ruin any chances of peace. Just goes to show ya', anytime those in power, like the governor or the Major, are lookin' to make their way by becomin' politicians, ain't none of 'em can be trusted!"

Reuben frowned, "Politicians?"

"Sure, didn't you know? Why ol' Evans has his cap set on bein' a senator and Chivington wants to be a congressman! But they figger they gotta settle this Indian thing, as they call it, or ain't nobody gonna support 'em! What with the war still goin' on back east and such, seems like folks want leaders they can trust and can end wars instead o' startin' 'em!" answered Bent, shaking his head and tossing out the dregs of his coffee again.

He stood, glanced at the sun and back to Reuben, "So, if you're gonna be workin' with me and tryin' to make some peace, I reckon y'all oughta be stayin' around." He pointed to the farthest hide lodge, "That lodge yonder is empty an' you're welcome to use it while you're here. So, go 'head on an' make youse'f ta home, and we'll visit again 'fore anything else happens." He pointed to the river crossing just above the confluence, "There's a rider comin' and I'm guessin' he's got news. So, we'll get together 'fore nightfall."

Reuben glanced at the rider and back to Bent,

nodded, and said, "We'll follow your lead!" and took Elly's arm and pointed her to the lodge. "You check out the lodge, I'll get the horses and pack mule." He watched as his woman and her dog walked casually among the Cheyenne and made her way to the tipi. He grinned as he watched her duck into the lodge and disappear.

5 / CONSIDERATIONS

The dim light of dusk shrouded the hide lodges, the stockade walls cast long but vague shadows down the slope toward the bosque, as William Bent came from the house and made his way to the lodge of Reuben and Elly. They had a small fire going in the center of the lodge, providing warmth as the night cooled, and light as both Reuben and Elly cleaned their weapons. A scratch at the blanket that hung at the opening heralded the greeting from Bent, "Ho, the lodge. Tis me, Bent, and I've got news."

"Come on in and join us!" answered Reuben, finishing a last swipe of the barrel of his Sharps, and removing the long swiping stick. He nodded to the buffalo hide that lay opposite the fire and watched as Bent dropped and found a comfortable seat.

With a nod to Elly, Bent looked at Reuben and began, "There were some troops that came from up by Castle Rock, and they told 'bout a couple attacks up north. Seems Powder Face an' Whirlwind led some Cheyenne and Arapaho in a strike at Jimmy's Camp. Stole some livestock, killed a feller by the name of Coberly, he had him a ranch up thataway. An' there was some others, they thought it was Kiowa and Comanche, but it's a little far north for them, what jumped a wagon and killed a man an' his son, stole the stuff and burnt the wagon."

"I haven't heard anything about a Powder Face an' Whirlwind. They some kinda war chiefs or sumpin'?" asked Reuben, frowning, and accepting a cup of steaming coffee from Elly.

"Naw, just a couple wannabe's tryin' to make a name for themselves." He also accepted a cup, brought it close and blew on the dark brew, tried taking a sip and made a face because it was hot. With a glance and a smile to Elly, he continued, "But that ain't all. Had some freighters come into the fort and tol' 'bout an attack on the trail west o' here. They was certain they was Kiowa and Comanche. Said there was ten men killed, bodies mutilated, an' their wagon's burnt. These fellas came on the wagons after the attack, but they said there was plenty sign o' Kiowa an' Comanche. Now what zackly they saw, I dunno, but they seemed mighty certain." He paused, tested the coffee again and took a long sip.

Reuben dropped his gaze to the fire, shaking his head, "Arapaho, Cheyenne, Dog Soldiers and Sioux, Kiowa and Comanche, sounds like it's happenin' all over." He lifted his eyes to Bent, "And that's just this past week. When you add in all the happenin's the week 'fore that, it's beginnin' to sound like an all-out war!"

"But it ain't just the natives! There's been several attacks by the troops under Chivington, Curtis, and more. The onliest one that ain't done any attackin' is Wynkoop, an' he's been tryin' to negotiate a peace!" proclaimed Bent, angrily, grabbing at a stick and tossing it into the fire. He shook his head, "And Black Kettle has

31

been doin' ever'thing he can to get the natives to make peace!"

Silence hung between them for a moment until Reuben spoke softly as he looked at Bent, "What can we do?" nodding to Elly and back to Bent.

Bent looked from Reuben to Elly and back, glanced around the tipi to give himself a moment to think, looked back to Reuben, "You're friends with Little Raven, right?"

"Ummhmm," replied Reuben, choosing to let Bent ponder and consider before saying any more.

"Maybe you can go see him, and maybe he can talk to some others." He paused, took another sip of coffee, "Here's what I'm thinkin'. I know Black Kettle wants to get the chiefs together and try to hammer out some kinda agreement for peace, kinda like he done with the Kiowa and Comanche before. I'll go see him, maybe sit with him as he meets with the others, an' help what I can. Little Raven and Left Hand have a lot of influence among the Arapaho, and they might get the Cheyenne, maybe War Bonnet, White Antelope, maybe One Eye. And if he can get the Cheyenne Dog Soldiers, prob'ly Bull Bear and Tall Bull, maybe even Eagle Head, maybe we can get some kinda agreement." He leaned back, sipped his coffee as his brow furrowed in thought. With a glance at Reuben, "Whatcha think?"

"The only one I know is Little Raven, but he's a well-respected leader and we'll go talk to him. But as far as the others, I know absolutely nothing at all."

Bent chuckled, "Yeah, and it don't make no difference. Since you're an outsider, they wouldn't let you come to the council anyway. But the Cheyenne still consider me a sub-chief among them cuz o' my wives, so I can sit in on it all. Won't have much say, but I can listen and talk when asked. All you need to do is talk to Little Raven."

"I'll do that, but I also need to do a little checkin' on the stages and wagon trains on the trails. See if there's anything we can do about the hold-ups and attacks and such. If you can get the others together, maybe that'll solve both problems," declared Reuben, his hopefulness showing in his eyes.

"Well, if you follow the Santa Fe trail east a ways, you might run into some o' the stages and such before you need to head north to find Little Raven. Since there's no hurry, that'd give you a couple days or so on the trail 'fore you go see the Arapaho. Course there's always the possibility you might run into the other Little Raven, the chief's son, and his war party that 'pears to be doin' as much as the Dog Soldiers."

Reuben frowned, "His son?"

"Ummhmm, his son. And even though he's got the same name, he ain't nothin' like his daddy!"

"If given the chance, would he talk to me?" queried Reuben, trying to consider all possibilities.

"Mebbe, but if'n I was you, I wouldn't be takin' no chances that weren't necessary." He twisted around to face Reuben, "What'cha need to understand is the Cheyenne have all their warrior bands, the *Hotamétaneo'o* or Dog Warriors or what they are also known, Dog Soldiers. Then there's the *Hema'tanónėheo'o* or Bowstrings, sometimes called the Wolf Warriors. And others like the Contrary Warriors, the Crazy Dogs, Elk Warriors and Shield Warriors, but the strongest are the Dog Soldiers and the Bowstrings. Now each of these have their own leaders and sub-chiefs and they are independent of all the others and are not governed by the others. So, when Black Kettle wants to make peace, the

Dog Soldiers are not bound by any agreement he makes with the governor or soldier boys. That's why the Dogmen are makin' war on their own and don't wanna talk peace with any of the troopers. And I'm thinkin' that young Little Raven wants to show that his war party of Arapaho are just as bad as the Dogmen!"

Bent extended his cup for some more coffee and Elly readily filled it with the steaming black brew. He brought it to his lips, took a noisy sip and continued. "There are the northern Cheyenne and the southern Cheyenne, and each are made up of bands or what some would call tribes, and these are the bands that make up the council of forty-four. It gets kind of complicated, but basically each band is independent of the other and acts alone, which makes it hard to negotiate a peace treaty unless they're all there."

He paused, chuckled, "So, enough about that, and that doesn't even include all the allies like the Lakota and the Arapaho." He took another sip to finish off the coffee, looked around the lodge and stood. Handing the cup to Elly he looked to Reuben, "So, I'm gonna leave in the mornin' to go see Black Kettle and try to help him with the other tribes and get some kinda peace goin', and if you talk to Little Raven, maybe they can get together with the others and see what happens."

Reuben stood, looking at Bent and agreed, "Then we'll be leavin' in the mornin' and travel downstream, talk to any freighters, wagons, and stages and see who's makin' war and causin' problems. If there's anything we can do, well, we'll just take it one day at a time and see," he mused, looking at Bent for any suggestions.

Bent extended his hand, nodding and grinning, "Now you see what we've been up against down here, and that doesn't even account for the politicians and soldier boys!"

Reuben nodded, shaking hands with the man, and glancing to his woman and back. "We'll check back with you first chance we get."

"You do that, and hopefully, I'll be back here instead of out there," answered Bent, nodding to the north where most of the camps of the natives lay.

6 / VISIT

"Is that smoke?" asked Elly, glancing to her left at Reuben. She nodded to the east further down the trail where a pair of rocky topped buttes rose as the rare break in the usual flatlands. They had been on the trail for a couple hours and the sun was just high enough to be out of their eyes and to reveal the scattered pillars of smoke beyond the nearest butte.

Reuben shaded his eyes as he pulled down the brim of his hat and stared into the distance. He frowned, keeping his eyes on the smoke, "Could be a village, but... I dunno. A village usually has a few thin tendrils of smoke, not the bigger stuff like that." He paused as he stood in his stirrups, an action that often helped but was usually more of a reflex in the effort to see just a little further. He looked to his left at the long line of green, cottonwoods, alders, and willows, that marked the banks of the Arkansas, and to his right at the long flat plains with the pale brown of the buffalo grass and random spots of blue/grey that told of clusters of sage.

He dropped into his saddle, pointed with his chin, "Let's go to the right of that butte, away from the trail.

Whatever that is, I don't think it's good. I got that feelin'," he explained. It was a feeling that many in the wilderness knew well when the hair on your neck bristled and the emptiness between your shoulder blades sent a clawing sensation into your gut to warn of something bad coming your way. Elly nodded and reined Daisy, her leopard appaloosa mare, away from the trail.

They were about two hours or about twenty miles from Fort Lyon and Bent's ranch. With those two hours on the trail, they were bound for the encampment of Little Raven and the Arapaho people of his band, but trouble on the trail piqued their curiosity and reminded them of their purpose for being in this part of Colorado Territory, a mission from Governor Evans. As they approached the base of the rocky topped butte, a small cluster of junipers offered a touch of shade and Reuben nodded as he reined up and swung down. He had his Sharps in hand, the binoculars in their case over one shoulder, and his possibles bag hung on the other. Elly stepped down, found a seat in the shade, and held the long leads of the two horses and mule, nodding to Reuben as he started up the butte. She was well familiar with his penchant of seeking out the high country to have his look around, but it was a trait she appreciated for it was one that kept them safe, or as safe as possible in a wild land.

He bellied down as he reached the crest and crabbed his way to a big rock for cover. Laying his Sharps to his side, he brought out the binoculars and began his scan. Below him, situated between this butte and another slightly taller one, was a collection of about fifteen wagons, formed up into a bit of a circle, with three wagons, or the remains of them, still smoldering. Scattered about around the perimeter of the circle were some dead horses and other sign that showed there were some of the attackers that had been killed or wounded. He counted what could have been at least five attackers killed, but the natives almost always retrieved their dead before leaving the site of the battle. While within the circle, the people were milling about, and as near as he could tell, they had also suffered some dead and wounded that were being tended to by the others. He frowned as he looked, adjusted his binoculars, and slowly searched the circle of wagons. The teams of mules were within the circle and were moving around, but what had caught his attention, was the appearance of the people. He frowned again, dropped the glasses as he looked and thought, lifted them again, and muttered, "Well, I'll be hornswoggled! Ever' one o' them is..." He took a deep breath, looked again, and searched the surrounding terrain for any sign of the attackers, but seeing none, he crabbed back from his perch and returned to the juniper cluster and Elly.

He was shaking his head and grinning as he neared and lifting his eyes to Elly, "Ain't never seen the like!"

"What'chu mean?" she asked, standing, and looking at her man. Bear rose to his feet beside her and leaned against her leg to assure her of his presence. She absently reached down to ruffle his scruff and frowned at Reuben, waiting for an answer.

"Well, it's a wagon train alright. They been hit by Indians and looks to be three of 'em burnt. But that's not the thing, that entire train is coloreds!"

"Coloreds? You mean..." and left the question hanging between them as she looked at her grinning husband, who nodded his answer.

"Well, that's different." She watched Reuben swing

aboard and she followed. Once aboard, she looked at him and asked, "Now what?"

"We'll go see what we can do to help. It appears they had some killed, others wounded, and they might need some help. I don't think the attackers will return, at least I couldn't see any sign of 'em anywhere, but..."

As they rode into sight of the wagons, most of the people were busy with their repairs and such, but a boy of about twelve with high-water britches held up by one strap, bare feet showing, and big eyes looking, saw them and hollered the alarm, prompting several of the men, rifles in hand to come to the perimeter and take cover. With rifles pointed at them, Reuben lifted his free hand, hollered out, "We're friendly! Comin' to help if we can!" Elly also lifted her free hand, and both reined up, waiting for a response from the people.

"What'chu want?" came the reply, one of the men standing to show himself.

"Can we come closer and talk?" asked Reuben.

"Come ahead on but keep yo' han's high!" answered the man, turning to his companions and speaking low to tell them to keep the visitors under guard.

As they neared, the speaker stepped over the tongue of one of the burnt wagons and walked forward. He was a big man, just over six feet tall, broad shouldered and standing proud. Grey showed at his temples, but his beard and hair were thick and black. He cradled a Sharps rifle in his arms, but his stoic expression showed nothing. He looked from Reuben to Elly, glanced at the big black dog beside the appaloosa, and back to Reuben, "I'm Moses Wright, I'm the wagonmaster, and you?"

"I'm Reuben Grundy and this is my wife, Elly," answered Reuben, leaning forward to cross his arms and lean on the saddle horn. "Looks like you folks had a little scrape with the natives."

"Ummhmm, you might call it dat. We run 'em off, though. Don't reckon they'll be comin' back."

"You lose many?" asked Reuben, looking at the wagonmaster and trying to read his responses.

"Three kilt, two wounded. We done more'n that to them." He paused, looking from Elly to Reuben, "But they took some," he added, dropping his head and his voice.

"Took some?" asked Reuben, lifting his head, and looking hard at the man.

"They was some young'uns down by the crik, they took 'em," grumbled the big man, his expression going from mistrust to sadness.

"How many?"

"Fo', two 'bout fo'teen or so, twins at lebben."

"Girls, boys?"

"All girls. Reckon dey be gone now," grumbled the man, as Reuben watched the others, still behind the circle of wagons but standing and listening, each one dropping their eyes and slowly shaking their heads.

Reuben breathed deep, gathering himself and stifling his anger, "When did they take 'em, how long ago?"

"Reckon it was durin' th'attack. Sho'tly after sunup."

"How long did the fight last?" asked Reuben, his nostrils flaring. Nothing got his ire up more than hearing of captives of the natives. He had gone against greater odds time and again to rescue captives. First against the plains tribes on the way west, then against the Comanche more recently. Before the man could answer, he asked, "Alright if I get down? I'd like to take a look at them," nodding to the horses of the attackers that lay sprawled away from the wagons.

"What fo' you wants to look at them?" asked the big man, frowning.

"I want to see who attacked you. That might tell us where they went."

The man frowned but walked beside Reuben as they started to the carcasses of the horses that had already attracted some carrion eaters, turkey buzzards, crows, magpies, two coyotes, and a badger. Reuben shouted and waved his hands to chase the animals away and drew near the carcass of a paint horse. He looked at the animal, the rigging, bridle, and markings. He looked up at Moses, "I think they were Comanche."

"Them whut attacked us?" asked Moses.

"That's right. This is their territory, well, them and the Kiowa mostly. But those markings," pointing to the jagged yellow line that portrayed lightning, and the handprint that told of its owner, "look more like Comanche."

Reuben stood and started back to the wagons, "The Comanche are big on taking women and girls captive, making them slaves, or taking them as wives. Some of the warriors already have a wife or two and any captives become the slaves of the women. But if it's a young warrior and he doesn't have a wife, he'll take her as his woman and if she suits him, he'll make her his wife."

"But the young'uns?"

"Sometimes they're taken or adopted as children of the warrior and his women, sometimes, even that young, they make them wives or slaves. Depends on their captors."

The big man shook his head as they walked, "We done come all dis way to get away from slavery an' now..."

41

When they came to the horses, Elly looked at her man and asked, "Who?"

"Comanche!" growled Reuben.

"And?"

"Goin' after 'em. You?"

"You ain't goin' nowhere without me!" declared Elly, grinning at her man.

7 / COMANCHE

"You're goin' after 'em?" asked Moses, eyes wide and surprise showing.

"That's right. I can't abide the Comanche always takin' captives. Gone against 'em before, just won't tolerate it!" declared Reuben as he swung back aboard Blue.

"Wait, wait. If you's goin', there's a couple men what would wanna come too. They be the pap's o' them girls! They gots a right!" declared Moses as he turned and motioned to one of the men to fetch the others.

"We ain't gonna be babysittin' no greenhorns. That'll just slow us down!" declared Reuben. He looked at Moses, "You keep these wagons movin'. You're only 'bout a day from Fort Lyon and you can wait there till we return."

"How long?" asked Moses, looking from Reuben and back to the wagons, anxious for the other men.

"Don't know. Maybe a couple days, maybe a week."

Two other men came at a run, rifles in hand, packs over their backs and waving at the wagonmaster. Moses looked at Reuben, "Could'ju wait?" nodding toward the two men.

Reuben looked at the runners, glanced at Elly and back to Moses. As the men jumped over the tongue of the wagon, they came to Moses side and one asked, "We goin' after 'em?"

"He is," answered Moses, nodding to Reuben.

"But, but, we needs ta' go, too!" declared the man.

Moses looked from one to the other and up at Reuben, he nodded to the first man, "This here's Gideon, he's the daddy o' them twins. An' this'n is Raphael, his girl is Dinah, the oldest."

Reuben looked from one to the other, back to Moses, "What about the father of the other girl?"

"He was kilt."

Reuben looked at the two fathers, "You men have horses?"

The men looked at one another, then to Moses. The wagonmaster answered, "We can gets 'em mounted, if'n you'll let 'em come wit'!"

Reuben looked at the men, then to the rifles. One carried a Sharps, the other had a Spencer. "Those are fine rifles; you know how to use them?"

Gideon held the Sharps and answered, "Yassuh, I was in Comp'ny B, Michigan, of Second U.S. Sharpshooters in the Union army!" declared the man, prompting Reuben to lift his eyebrows and show his surprise.

"And you?" looking to the man with the Spencer known as Raphael.

"I was in the 54th Massachusetts under Colonel Shaw till I gots shot."

"The 54th was an infantry unit, can you ride?"

Raphael chuckled, "If'n it's got legs, I c'n ride it!"

Moses had sent one of the other men to fetch mounts and he returned leading two saddled mules, both bays, and both carrying a bedroll and stuffed saddle bags. At Moses nod, the two men swung aboard and looked to Reuben.

Reuben glanced to Elly, shrugged, and pointed Blue to the tracks of the Comanche, waving Bear to take point as they began their search for the attackers. The trail took an angle to the southwest, moving across the flats toward the headwaters of the Purgatoire River. The terrain where they were was mostly flat to rolling land, clusters of sage, greasewood, and rabbit brush breaking the monotony of the mostly dusty brown land with the buffalo and bunch grasses giving the only color. This was a land inhabited by jackrabbits, coyotes, lizards, and rattlesnakes, with the only meat animal being the skittish pronghorns whose eyesight was six times better than man's and his speed faster than the new locomotives back east.

They had traveled but a short distance when Reuben leaned over to Elly, he handed the lead to the pack mule to her and said, "You take the lead, I'm gonna drop back and learn a little more about our new additions."

Elly nodded and watched as Reuben pulled up to wait for the two mule riders to come alongside. He nudged Blue closer to mule ridden by Raphael and began, "Tell me about the wagon train, where 'bouts you folks headed?"

"Don't rightly know. Moses said we'd know it when we see'd it. He's been out thisaway 'fore, but he ain't seen it all. He's talked a lot 'bout Colorado Terr'try, but we just be trustin' him," answered Raphael with a glance to Gideon.

"You see much action with the 54th?"

"Some, 'nuff to get shot! That was at Grimball's Landing, more'n a year'go. Mustered out and joined up wit' Moses, he was wit' th' First Kansas."

"All the men with the wagons fight in the war?" asked Reuben.

"Most of'm," answered Raphael, looking to Gideon for confirmation.

Gideon nodded his head, keeping his silence, until Reuben looked at him and asked, "You were a sharpshooter, huh?" He paused to see the man nod, then continued, "I was with Berdan's Sharpshooters."

Gideon's expression changed, breaking into a grin and a nod, "They was the fust!"

"Ummhmm. We saw quite a bit of action, leastways till I was so weighted down with lead they thought they better let me go home," answered Reuben. He looked directly at Gideon, "You got a scope for that Sharps?"

Gideon patted the saddle bags that hung behind his McClellan saddle and nodded his head.

"Then we might be doin' some long-distance shooting. Depends on what we find when we catch up to 'em."

Raphael looked at Reuben, glanced up to Elly and asked, "Have you fought the Comanche 'fore?"

Reuben chuckled, "Yup. The Pawnee, Cheyenne, Arapaho, Ute, Apache, and Comanche. But me'n the Comanche, well, let's just say we don't get along too well."

"Why's dat?" asked Raphael.

Reuben nodded towards Elly, "'Bout a year ago, they took her captive, and several of our neighbors' wives and girls. When I went to get them back, had to do a bit o' killin', just so's they'd remember. But 'pears they done forgot."

Raphael looked to Gideon and back to Reuben, "So, she'll be fightin', too?"

"It'd be a bigger fight to keep her out of it!" chuckled Reuben. He nudged Blue ahead to catch up with Elly and pulled up alongside her, smiling at her as she looked at him.

"So, what's got you to grinnin'?" she asked.

He nodded toward the two men, "They asked if you were gonna be doin' any fightin' and I said it'd be a bigger fight to keep you out of it!"

"That's for certain!" she declared. "I never did get my 'pound of flesh' from the last time!" As she spoke, she frowned, stood in her stirrups, and nodded ahead. "What's that about?"

A flock of turkey buzzards were circling high above the flats and beyond the sage, it appeared there were some carrion eaters attacking something on the ground. They had come about fifteen miles from the site of the wagons and the rolling plains offered little cover, but they continued ahead, watchful for any possible ambush. Bear came trotting back toward them, stood in the middle of the trail, his tongue lolling and his stance showing no give at all. Reuben and Elly reined up and Elly called, "Bear, come here." The big dog trotted to her side, and they nudged their mounts forward, moving closer to the kill, fearful of what they would find.

As they neared, Reuben stopped, turned to the men, "You men wait here. Stay ready and watchful. I'm goin' to have a look-see." With a nod to Elly, Reuben swung down, slipping the Henry from the scabbard and with a motion to Bear, the two started to the kill that had attracted the carrion. They charged forward at a run, shouting, and waving his arms, Bear barking, and the coyotes scattered, the buzzards hopping away just out of reach.

As he feared, it was the body of one of the captives. She had been mutilated after she was killed, but the carrion had done so much damage, it was impossible to tell just what caused her death, until he stepped closer and dropped to one knee to see the clean cut of a knife that slit her throat. Sightless eyes stared at the cloudless sky, her scalp taken and leaving the bloody skin and bone of her skull exposed. The buzzards had yet to go for the eyes, but her stomach had been ripped open and her lower neck had been gouged. Reuben looked away, glanced toward the others, and looked to Bear. "Keep 'em away, boy. I'll be right back."

He returned to the horses, his jaw muscles flexing as he gritted his teeth to keep his stomach contents down and took an extra blanket from the packs on the mule. He looked at Raphael, "You need to come with me."

As the man sided Reuben, he asked, "Is it my Dinah?"

"I dunno. But it's one of the girls. You need to steel yourself before you look." Reuben stopped, turning to face the man, and said, "It won't be easy, but it needs to be done. Are you ready?"

Raphael nodded, turned toward the body, and started forward. As he neared, he paused, stumbled, and fell to his knees beside the girl, reaching out to touch her shoulder. His head dropped and his shoulders heaved. He turned away and regurgitated, wiping his face with the back of his hands as he stood and lifted his arms to the sky and wailed, "Nooooooooo!" He looked back at the body, glanced to Reuben, and nodded, "It's my Dinah." He turned away again, shaking his head, and stubbing his toe in the dirt as his shoulders shook with his sobbing.

Reuben carefully and respectfully wrapped the girl's body in the blanket, lifted her from the ground and spoke softly to Raphael, "We need to get busy burying her."

8 / CHASE

With the shovel from the pack mule, Reuben made short work of digging the grave. While he labored with the shovel, the two men gathered rocks for covering the burial. They knew they were pressed for time, but the grieving father lingered as long as he could, outstretched on the grave as if he could hold his child one more time. Reuben dug his Bible from his saddle bags and stood before the crude headstone, "Psalm 91 says, *For He shall give His angels charge over thee, to keep thee in all thy ways.* And a little further on, *Because he hath set his love upon me, therefore will I deliver him: I will set him on high, because he hath known my name.*" He looked from Raphael to Gideon and to Elly, "Let's pray. Our Father in Heaven, we surrender our sister, Dinah, to you and the angels of Heaven. We ask that you reach down and give comfort to Raphael and Dinah's mother as they grieve for the loss of their child. Now go before us as we seek to find and rescue the other girls. We thank you in Jesus' name, Amen."

Reuben nodded to Elly and Gideon and turned back to the horses, reached down to tug on Raphael's shoulder for him to come along. The man looked up at Reuben, back at the grave and struggled to his feet. Wiping his tears away with his sleeve, he walked beside Reuben, paused and turned to face him, "That verse you read, I recomember it some. My mammy used to read it to us." He paused, frowning, "The way I heerd it, they was another verse whut said, uh, *Wit' yo eyes will yo see da reward o' th' wicked.*" He looked at Reuben, "Don't it?"

Reuben flipped the pages back to Psalm 91 and nodded, then read, *"Only with thine eyes shalt thou behold and see the reward of the wicked."*

"Ummhmm. Le's be bringing da' reward to dem wicked Comanche!" declared Raphael as he swung aboard his mule.

Reuben nodded and stepped aboard Blue, motioned to Bear to take the lead and follow the trail, and dug heels to the big roan. Elly sided him and the two men followed close behind with the pack mule pushing up on the far side of Blue. The mule and Blue had become traveling partners and it was not uncommon for Reuben to let the mule follow free rein, but with the trail uncertain and the danger that awaited, he wanted the animal under close control.

In the distance, long lines of flat-topped mesas marked the western horizon with random buttes and bluffs showing themselves closer. Reuben left the obvious trail of the Comanche, taking up their pursuit parallel to the trail but separated by about fifty yards. He knew Bear could keep on their tracks, but if the warriors had one of their number drop back and watch their back trail, he did not want it obvious they were following. The reports from the two men and the obvious sign of the tracks told there were about twenty warriors in the war party and with that number, he knew they would not be afraid of anyone that would follow or any others they might encounter.

Although the army could field a company or even brigade that could number in the hundreds, any of those were already busy with the attacks closer to Denver City where the populace had demanded the army provide protection from the warring Indians. The nearest company of soldiers were those at Fort Lyon, and with their commander, Major Wynkoop, getting conflicting orders from the governor, General Curtis, and Colonel Chivington, he sought to make peace rather than send out a punitive force against any of the natives. Reuben had become well versed in the ways and plans of the politicians and commanders by Bent and knew if anything was to be done about the Comanche attack, it would be entirely up to him and those with him.

They were riding into the setting sun and the terrain was changing. As they neared the channel of the Purgatoire, crossing some of the feeder draws, the shadows stretched long, and the terrain showed an abundance of buttes, mesas, and sandstone cliffs. The juniper, piñon, and cedar were becoming abundant. The rocky banks of the river were obscured by the thick willows and alder. Even the cholla, prickly pear, and bunch grass grew tall. Reuben reined up beside a cluster of tall juniper and stepped down, motioning the others to do the same.

"We're gonna take a break, get the animals some water, maybe let 'em roll and get some grass. We'll get us some food, but it'll be a cold camp. The sky is clear and with the moon waxin' full, it'll be light enough for us to move out after sunset," explained Reuben as he went to the mule to fetch one of the parfleche that had smoked meat.

"How far we gots to go?" asked Raphael, stripping the saddle from his mule.

"I don't think they're more'n an hour or two away, if that far. I think they might be a little overconfident, although that'd be rare for the Comanche, but I think we can catch up to 'em after dark."

"You mean we'll hit 'em in the dark?" asked Gideon, a little incredulous.

"Didn't you do any night huntin' with the 2nd?"

"Uh, yeah. But..."

"But what? Dark is dark, and with the moonlight tonight, I think we can do alright. Just follow my lead cuz Comanche are a lot different than the Confederates. They don't sleep as sound and they always have lookouts," added Reuben.

"I'se just worried 'bout muh babies," explained Gideon.

"We all are, and we'll do everything we can to make sure they're safe," explained Reuben, "So, let's get us somethin' to eat, maybe a bit of rest, and we'll move out soon."

They sat back against a big sandstone boulder, watching the sunset as the Creator painted the sky with shafts of gold, orange and red and as the sun lowered itself below the horizon, the shadows of the earlier colors added a tinge of deep purple as the golden orb bid its goodnight. The stars lit their lanterns, one at a time, and began to decorate the summer sky with a myriad of sparkles that elicited a few oohs and ahhhs from the observers. With the sun gone, the night air cooled, and Reuben stood, nodding to the horses, "It's time we got 'em rigged."

With a deep breath of the night air that was flavored with juniper berries, wilted prickly pear blossoms and yucca blossoms, and the muted smell of piñon and cedar, Reuben looked heavenward and smiled, mumbled a quiet "Thank you Lord," and saddled his roan. As Elly put the rest of the dried meat back into the parfleche and carried it to the pack mule, Reuben had finished rigging the pack saddle and packs, accepting the parfleche and secured the load. He saddled the Appaloosa for Elly, looked to the men, and saw their mounts were rigged and ready, and walked closer.

"When we find their camp, we'll probably split up. You two will go one way," and with a nod to Elly, "We'll go another. Depending on their camp, I'll scout it out, and return with a plan and we'll do as it looks best. We're outnumbered, but with surprise, good cover, and good shooting, I think we'll get the job done." He paused, looked at each of the men, "I know you're anxious to get some revenge," looking directly at Raphael, and turned to Gideon, "And you're anxious to get your daughters back. But if you try to do it on your own, you'll prob'ly get killed and maybe the rest of us too. We've fought these Comanche before and they're fierce warriors. The last thing you want to happen is to be taken by them. As fighters, you'll get no mercy. I've known them to tie their captives to a tree and burn them and the tree to the ground, after they torture you for a day or two." He paused to let his warning take root, and continued, "So, don't go losin' control and wade into 'em. Got it?" He looked from one to the other, watched as each one eagerly nodded their head in agreement.

"Alright, let's move out. No talkin' and stay close," he admonished as he stepped aboard the roan.

While the rest were eating, Reuben had made a scout on foot, searching out the tracks of the war party, trying to determine what they were prone to do, and after his scout, and his scan from the top of the butte by the dim light of dusk, he had formulated a bit of a plan. Believing the war party had chosen a camp in a rocky canyon about five or six miles away, he led the way on a wide swinging route that would take them to the far side of their camp. Believing that if they expected any attack, they would expect it to come from their back trail, not the trail between them and their village.

They moved away from the area of random buttes, making their way across an open flat that carried a small feeder creek that served the Purgatoire. Reuben was uncomfortable, continually looking around across the flats that showed few shadows of sage and greasewood. The cicadas rattled their wings, a distant coyote lifted his cry to the moon, and as they neared the creek, the croak of a pair of competing bullfrogs was muffled by the dry willows. They were near the trail of the Comanche and used the same crossing that was peppered with the tracks of the war party, but once above the creek and on the flats, Reuben moved away from the obvious tracks of the Comanche.

Standing tall and stretching across the western horizon, rose the many wide mesas with juniper, cedar, and piñon hugging their flanks. Reuben found himself holding his breath as he nudged Blue into a trot to get to the safety of the flat-tops and the trees. Once in the protection of cover, he relaxed and let the others come alongside. In a low voice he explained, "We'll get back on their trail," nodding his head in the direction of the worn path, "this area is full of arroyos and ravines that could swallow the whole bunch of us, and we wouldn't find our way out till sometime next winter. But we'll follow their sign until it appears they are lookin' for a camp.

Then we'll move away and search things out a little better and under cover of darkness."

The men nodded and Reuben looked to Elly to see her smiling and confident face as she gave a slight nod as well. Once again, he motioned Bear to the trail and the four followed as they started up a slanting trail that took them to the top of a long plateau. Once atop the flat, they stretched out in single file, keeping to the trail but ever watchful. With a glance to the stars, Reuben guessed it to be crowding midnight, and looked ahead into the dim light to try to judge the trail. To his right, arroyos clawed their way to the lower reaches of the headwaters of the Purgatoire, each carrying runoff in the early spring, but now showing only shadows of juniper, cedar, and piñon, but they beckoned with cover and shelter. He was getting jittery being exposed with little or no cover save that skeletal cholla and buffalo grass, neither big enough to hide a man, much less several people on horseback.

As he looked around, the shadowy figure of Bear trotted back toward them, stopped, and dropped to his haunches in the middle of the trail. As they neared the big dog, he came to his feet, looked back up the trail, and growled. Reuben squinted, trying hard to pierce the dim light with his eyes, but failing. He glanced to Elly who nodded toward the nearby arroyo, and he nodded, nudging Blue toward the tree filled draw. They dropped over the edge into the draw, finding a flat that held one of the rare springs that bubbled out from under a big sandstone boulder, and Reuben spoke softly, "We'll stop here. I think I'll make a scout on foot." He stepped down, led the roan to the water and loosened the girth. Dropping the reins to ground tie the big roan, he slipped the Henry from the scabbard and stepped beside Elly, "I'm takin' Bear, so you keep watch, but stay under cover and keep your rifle handy. I'll be back as soon as I can, just don't shoot me when I do!" he chuckled, knowing Elly was always cautious, more than most.

"You just make sure you come back!" she ordered, slipping her Henry from the scabbard. Reuben grinned, slipped on his moccasins and nodded, looked to the men, "I'll be back soon. Stay watchful!" and disappeared into the dark trees.

9 / AMBUSH

The moon was waxing toward full and was just past half, the big crescent hanging high above the silhouetted mountains like a giant bowl, waiting to be filled by the magical potion of the sparkling stars. Having marked the point where the tracks of the Comanche had entered the trees and ravines of the foothills, Reuben pushed his way quietly through the juniper and cedar, shying clear of the rubble that lay at the base of each of the trees. He felt as much as watched where he was going, the soft soled moccasins warning of any noisemakers that might fall underfoot.

The soft blue of the moon lanced through the trees, lighting his way with freckled pools of moonlight. He stealthily moved, listening, watching, and smelling the air for smoke or any other giveaway like bear grease in the hair of the warriors or lathered horses. With a mile behind him, the trees were thicker, and the deep shadow of an arroyo showed ahead. Sandstone formations and cliffs caught the moonlight and stood as both a beacon and warning, but he smelled smoke, and the stifling wet from the fire being doused.

Reuben went to one knee, staying beside a twisted cedar, searching the area nearby and the open space above the rimrock on the far side. Below in the arroyo, deep shadows masked the camp, but he bellied down and moved closer to the edge of the sandstone precipice. Careful not to scrape anything on the loose gravel and rough faced sandstone, knowing the slightest movement could give a warning sound in the night when sound carries in the clear air. He lay still, searching below at what began to reveal itself as the camp of the Comanche. He breathed slowly, moving only his eyes, his arms beside him, elbows cocked for quick movement, hands spread wide for stability, toes on solid footing. Minutes slowly ticked in his mind as he mentally mapped the entire camp, at least what he could make out. Directly below him, huddled figures shared a single blanket and Reuben knew that bundle was the three girls. Close beside them, a single warrior lay on his back, but as he rolled to his side, his arm showed a tether tied to the ankle of one of the girls. Reuben shook his head, but scanned the rest of the camp, wanting to spot any lookouts.

As he searched through slitted eyes, he felt a tickle on his right hand and cautiously looked down without moving his head to see a long-legged hairy tarantula stretching multi-colored legs out to test the impediment to his journey. The spider was larger than the span of Reuben's hand, but he could not move for the bite of the big wanderer could be deadly. He forced himself to slow his breathing, watching the long legs reaching out, touching, then pulling himself along. Reuben's shadow covered the spider, but he could feel the long legs and hard tips as he moved across his hand working toward his face. The tarsal claws digging into his flesh for footing, fangs clinching and opening, two beady eyes looked at Reuben as if inspecting this strange but warm rock he was climbing upon. The spider paused, legs and claws testing the flesh, then slowly moved off the back of his hand, turned away and disappeared into the darkness.

Reuben breathed deep, for he had not realized he had been holding his breath, but relief washed over him, and he looked below at the encampment. Moving slowly and silently back from the edge and into the shadow of the twisted cedar, he came to his feet. With another scan of the nearby terrain, he started into the trees, his form whispering into the darkness like other phantoms of the night. A chill ran up his back as he remembered the spider, shook his head and muttered a silent prayer of thankfulness that it had not been a snake, knowing he could not have stayed still while a rattlesnake crawled over his hand, but would probably have come up shooting. He shook his head, thinking how he hated snakes of any kind, a thought that went back to his childhood and his brothers always coming after him with snakes. He shivered again and stepped into a trot to return to the camp. A quick glance to the sky showed there was only about three hours of darkness left, maybe even a little less.

"What'd you find?" asked Gideon who had been standing in the trees away from the camp, watching for Reuben.

Reuben nodded, motioned for him to follow, and joined the others at the grassy flat of the campsite. A quick glance showed all the animals had been tethered and were standing hipshot, heads drooping, and quiet. The others drew near, and he began to explain in a low voice, "Their camp is just over a mile through the trees, and we've got a couple hours, maybe more of darkness, but this is the time when most are in their deepest sleep. So," he dropped down to the ground, motioned them back a step to let the moonlight show his drawing in the dirt, and began to explain what they would do as they formed their ambush of the Comanche. As he finished, "Now, the Comanche don't usually think there will be anyone that would dare attack one of their camps, but they'll still be cautious. So, we can't take any risks. Always move quietly, watch where you're steppin' and be sure of where you're goin'. And be especially wary of the sandstone, it can be deceptive, and you can easily topple a stone, slip on the sandy surface, and more." He looked from Gideon to Raphael, and with a nod to the men and a touch on Elly's arm, they started into the trees.

When still about a hundred yards from the Comanche camp, Reuben, who had chosen his Henry for the close in work and now carried it in the crook of his arm, pointed out the pre-selected routes and the two men started off. He turned to Elly, "The promontory I mentioned is straight ahead. From there you can see into the camp and pick your targets. Remember, the girls are near the cliff face to your right, but you'll be close enough to see them. Your job is to cover everything I didn't think of..." he grinned as he looked at her and heard her low chuckle. She shook her head, "That's askin' a lot of a girl," she said, patted her rifle, "but me'n Henry here should be alright."

"Just remember, I'll be on the upper end and in the trees!" he cautioned.

Reuben quickly disappeared into the trees and Elly took to the slight climb onto the sandstone that appeared like a stack of buff and red colored flat rocks. She would be atop the cliff near where Reuben had scouted the camp, Reuben would be in the trees on the

61

upper end of the camp and on the trail where the Comanche would normally choose to flee toward their village. Raphael would be on the far side of the arroyo, positioned to shoot down into the encampment. Gideon would go after the girls.

Reuben knew he would be the last one in position, and he would start any action, but first he had to locate the lookouts and try to eliminate as many as possible. As he drew near the upper end of the camp, he knew most warriors would choose to keep their horses near and would trust them to give any alarm of unwanted visitors. But Reuben had a way with horses and had made sure that Blue's scent was masking his own by hugging up on the horse before he left. He moved through the trees as silently as the night breeze, drawing closer to the sleeping forms. Moving from tree to tree, he watched for any movement and tested the air for any scent of bear grease that was used by the Comanche for their hair.

He caught a whiff of one, froze in place and watched until he spotted the figure, seated at the base of a big aspen. He grinned, for the man was easily spotted, his dark hair and skin standing in contrast to the white barked quaky. Reuben watched as the man's chin rested on his chest, breathing even, and with no other movement it told him that the man was asleep. Using the sling to secure his Henry, Reuben slipped his razor-sharp Bowie the scabbard at his back and moved behind the big aspen. As he drew close, he went to one knee, reached around the tree with his left hand, and cupped the man's mouth as he quickly drew the blade of the Bowie across his throat. The warrior kicked out, grabbing at Reuben's wrist, tried to breathe but sucked blood instead. Reuben's grip held him still until blood flowed over his arm and down the side of the warrior's chest and arm. When he was still, Reuben moved back into the shadows and wiping his hand and arm on a handful of damp leaves, he searched for another guard.

He was skillful at moving quietly through the woods and the darkness, a skill he mastered against those same brothers that had chased him with snakes. He had repeatedly gained his revenge in the many times they went into the woods for their jaunts of hunting and stalking one another. Now that skill was put to good use as he melted into the shadows, silently moving from darkness to darkness, avoiding the shafts of dim moonlight. Within moments, he spotted another guard that was moving toward the form of the man that appeared to be sleeping against the aspen. Reuben stepped between the trees, slipped his metal bladed tomahawk from his belt, and stepped forward as he threw the weapon. The blade flashed in the moonlight as it tumbled through the air to bury itself in the skull of the second guard, stifling any alarm as he crumpled to the ground. Reuben looked around for any sign of alarm, but there was none. He stepped to the carcass, jerking the hawk from the man's skull, and moved back into the shadows.

Reuben saw one of the horses lift his head quickly and let a low rumble come from his chest as he looked in the direction of the downed guard. Probably the smell of blood had alarmed the animal, but his movement awakened the man that lay nearby, and the warrior came to his feet, looking around. When he spotted the downed guard, he shouted the alarm and every warrior rolled from his blanket, coming to his feet, and searching the camp. The chatter of low voices filled the air as warriors looked about, searching for any attackers, holding rifles or bows or lances in their hands ready for any charge. But nothing came.

Reuben had faded back into the darkness, going to a pre-selected firing position, rifle in hand. Once at the upper end of the camp and beside a lone ponderosa that appeared to grow out of the moss-covered rock formation, he chose his first target, it was the first man who was moving toward the two downed guards. The Henry barked and the muzzle spat flame, smoke, and lead. The bullet found its mark and the warrior grabbed at his chest as his legs gave way and he dropped to his knees, trying to speak, and slowly lifting his rifle with one hand, but fell on his face. Reuben had already jacked another shell into the chamber and was picking his second target. Another warrior screamed, pointing to the trees and Reuben's bullet stopped his cry as it tore through his neck.

The big bark of the Spencer from the hands of Raphael came from the bluff above the camp on Reuben's right, another warrior stumbled backwards and vainly tried to keep his feet, but the .52 caliber lead slug bore him to the ground. A streak of flame and the bark of a Henry came from the cliff top to Reuben's left and he grinned as he knew Elly had chosen her target. Reuben jacked another shell as he moved through the shadows to another position, knowing each time he fired, the flame, smoke and report would give his position away and he moved quickly. Using the rough bark of another ponderosa as his side leaning rest, he fired again, taking another Comanche down. A second shot also scored, and he was on the move again.

Both Raphael and Elly had been cautioned to move often, not only to keep the Comanche from spotting their position, but to give the impression of more attackers. With Raphael's Spencer repeater, Elly's and Reuben's Henry repeaters, they laid down a barrage of thunder and lead on the surprised warriors who were taking to their horses and searching for a target or an escape. But the mounted warriors gave Elly an even better target and she repeatedly scored solid hits. Raphael also proved himself an able fighter as his Spencer barked again and again, every bullet drawing blood.

With a quick glance toward the cliffs, Reuben saw the shadowy figure of Gideon beside the girls and gesturing to the trail that would take them to the top of the cliff. He saw the man turn and saw his Sharps spit fire as it roared with an unmistakable thunder that was made even more intimidating as it echoed off the cliff face behind him. Reuben saw a mounted warrior, laying low on the neck of his mount, charging toward Gideon and he knew the Sharps required dexterity, skill, and time to reload. He snapped the Henry to his shoulder, drew a quick bead, and dropped the hammer. The mount stumbled, the warrior tumbling over his head to the ground but quickly coming to his feet. The man grabbed for his tomahawk, but Reuben fired again, taking the warrior low in the chest, and driving him to his knees. The feathered warrior turned to look toward Reuben with eyes flaring and a scream filling the air, but Elly's Henry bucked and barked and the slug tore through the man's scalplock and buried itself into his skull. The warrior fell to his face, dead.

Gideon had disappeared into the shadows of the cliff, chasing after the girls, and appeared to be out of reach of the warriors. Reuben turned back to the others, saw the ground was littered with the dead, and searched for another target. Three warriors, lying low on the necks of their mounts charged into the trees between Reuben and the cliff, taking the trail that would lead them deeper into the gorge and hills, probably to their village. He searched for other Comanche warriors, but there were none.

The cloud of rifle smoke lay low over the remains of the camp and the many bodies, the stench of burnt gun powder, blood, and excrement filled the air, but silence covered it all like a blanket of shadows retreating from the dim light of the thin grey line in the east that marked the slow rising sun. Reuben stepped from the trees, moving among the dead, lifted his eyes as Raphael came from the far side, also looking at the devastation. The men did not speak, both with faces dirtied by gun smoke and dirty hands wiping away sweat and even tears. They looked at one another, turned to face the cliff and saw Gideon and Elly flanking the three girls and looking down upon the two men. With an uplifted hand, Reuben forced a grin and a nod and both men moved to join the others.

10 / RETURN

"What about my Daddy?" asked Sarai, the oldest of the three girls. She and Raphael's daughter, Dinah, had been the best of friends. Her mother died before they left Missouri on the wagons and her father, Eustis, thought it best to get a fresh start in the west.

"He was kilt, missy," answered Raphael. Sarai was riding the mule behind him and lay her head against his back, letting the tears flow down her dirty face.

"I thot so," she answered, choking on the words and the effort to speak as her throat constricted with grief. She hugged herself tight against Raphael, "Whut am I gonna do now?" she cried, sniffling, and trying to wipe her tears with the corner of the blanket.

"You be stayin' wit' us," answered Raphael. "Dinah woulda liked dat."

"But, but, what if'n you gits kilt, too?" she sniffled.

"Ain't nobody gonna be killin' dis man. Uhuh, nossir. Ain't gonna be hap'nin," he declared, twisting in his saddle to look over his shoulder at the youngster. "You just rest easy, missy. Things gonna be alright now," he reassured.

The twins, Leah and Lydia, rode with their father, Gideon. One in front, the other behind. As Leah leaned back against her daddy, he held her close. Lydia hung on tight with her arms around the waist of the bigger man, her head resting on his back. Lydia asked, "We gonna be alright now, Daddy?"

"Yes'm, ain't nuthin' gonna happen to you agin! I won't let it!" he declared.

"Ain't there more injuns?" asked Leah, trying to look back at her dad.

"Lots o' 'em, but they ain't gonna git'chu!"

"I was skeered, daddy," mumbled Lydia, against her father's back.

"I was too, little'n. I was too. But da Lawd done sent us a couple angels to hep us, an' we done brought'chu back!"

"Will Jesus send another'n if he has too?" pleaded Lydia.

"Ummhmmm, but let's us just pray He don't haf'to!" chuckled Gideon, hugging his girls tight.

Reuben and Elly reined up, motioned for Gideon and Raphael to come alongside. As they neared, both Reuben and Elly turned to face them. Reuben nodded to the trail before them, "You just follow that that'away, and you'll come to Fort Lyon 'bout sundown. Moses said they'd be waiting there."

Gideon nudged the mule closer and stretched out a hand to Reuben, "Mistuh Reuben," and with a nod to Elly, "Missus Elly, you two done been angels fo' us. We be eternal grateful. Can't ever thank you 'nuff." He shook Reuben's hand, nudged his mule away to make room for Raphael.

Raphael came close and also extended his hand, "Ain't got wuds ta' say." He shook his head, fought back some tears, and wiped them away, "May da' good Lawd ride wit'chu!" he declared as he shook Reuben's hand. He glanced to Elly, "Missy, yo' a mahvel, yes'm. Like Gideon said, you two is angels, indeedy!"

Elly smiled, nodded, "You both are good men, and you take care of those girls, now, y'hear?" she chuckled, knowing the men would probably never let the youngsters out of their reach for a long time to come.

"Yes'm, we will," answered Raphael, glancing to a nodding Gideon.

Reuben looked at Raphael, "I never told you, but my brother's name was Raphael, and you've worn that name with honor. We're proud to have known you."

Reuben and Elly reined their mounts aside and watched the two men and the girls take to the trail. As they disappeared over the slight rise, Elly asked, "We goin' to see Little Raven now?"

"That's the idea, unless we get distracted again!" chuckled Reuben. He leaned over and pulled Elly close as they hugged one another, until the appaloosa stepped away, almost unseating Elly until she drew the reins tight and grabbed the saddle horn to pull herself back in the saddle. Both chuckled and Reuben said, "I reckon Daisy there might be anxious to see her friends again."

"And look at Bear, I'm thinkin' he's still a little put off about not gettin' in the fight last night."

"He'll get over it. I think we'll prob'ly have another fight or two to keep him busy." With a wave of his hand, he sent the big dog to scout the trail before them and they followed after.

Clay Creek was a shallow creek that twisted its way through the lowlands thick with willows and alders. A random cottonwood or two would raise their heads high above the undergrowth as if waving to passersby or to give sign to distant travelers that there was more to the prairie than cacti. With the meandering creek on their right, they pointed north, anxious to reach the Arkansas and make their crossing before they lost daylight. And it was the setting sun that painted the land with muted shades of pink, accompanied by the rattling cry of a pair of sandhill cranes and the screech of a snipe. Bear was startled by the loud cry of the long-legged crane and stopped with head lowered as he looked to the side of the trail into the tall willows to see a red headed crane casually walk from the brush, looking toward the creek, and apparently calling his mate.

Bear glanced back at the two riders, then trotted on, determined to lead the way. Within moments he came to the point of a peninsula that lay at the confluence of the creek and river and stood on the wet sand, looking across the river at something that caught his attention. He dropped into his attack stance, head lowered, feet spread, lip curling in a snarl and let a growl crawl from deep within. Reuben and Elly swung down, rifles in hand and moved to Bear's side, looking at the brush covered bank on the far side of the river. A small hunting party of about a dozen warriors rode the far bank, searching both sides of the river for game. Although Reuben and Elly were behind the cover of some thick willows, Bear was exposed until Elly whispered to call him back. He slowly backstepped, watching the Indians, and was soon hidden beside Elly in the brush.

Reuben slowly parted the thin willows, wanting to see what the party was doing and if they had been seen. The band continued to move, the leader motioning to the others, directing them to different points along the twisting riverbank, hopeful of finding game. It was the prime time for game, many deer, antelope, and even an occasional moose could be found near the water in this part of the country. With most of the herds of buffalo having already migrated north, it would be a while before they began their journey south. In the mid-summer months, most natives depended on deer, antelope, and small game for their meat.

"Arapaho!" whispered Reuben, "But none look familiar. Dunno if they're with Little Raven."

"Are we gonna cross, or wait?" whispered Elly, listening to the clatter of horses' hooves over the gurgle of the river.

"Let's just sit here a spell. I ain't too interested in spookin' a dozen natives when we don't have to!"

"Good idea," answered Elly, turning back to the horses and pack-mule. They were in good cover of a cluster of cottonwoods, some stretching skeletal dead grey branches through the umbrella of green. She fished through the parfleche for some dried meat and returned to Reuben's side with a handful.

He nodded, grinned, and started chewing on the smoke flavored tidbit. "A hot cup o' coffee'd sure taste good 'bout now."

"If you can make a little fire that doesn't smoke, doesn't smell, doesn't send up a pillar of embers to tell everybody where we are, and I'll fix you some."

"Oh, there ya' go, thinkin' practical again!" chuckled Reuben. "There's only a dozen of 'em. That'd be six apiece. We can handle that."

"That's quite alright. I've had enough killin' for a while if that's alright with you. 'Sides, they might be from Little Raven's camp, and he wouldn't take it too friendly if we killed a bunch o' his hunters."

"Then we'll give 'em a while 'fore we cross over. But I do want to get to th' other side 'fore dark!"

Dusk was beginning to fade when Reuben and Elly pushed their mounts into the water of the rippling river, choosing to cross above the confluence on what appeared to be a shallow and gravel bottomed crossing. Elly led and was digging her heels to the appaloosa to climb the far bank when Reuben and Blue approached the edge of the water. Just as Blue dug deep in the soft soil of the bank, the mule spooked and jerked the line from Reuben's hand, fighting the current and charging to the bank. Reuben looked over his right shoulder to see what spooked the mule and saw a young bull moose coming from the marsh beside the small fork that formed an island on the downstream side of the confluence. He slapped legs to Blue to come from the water and once on dry land, he swung down, Sharps in hand. He looked to Elly, "Grab the lead of the mule, I'm goin' after that moose!"

11 / MEAT

In the fading light, the big brown beast looked gangly and awkward, wet greens hanging from his antlers, big lips and nose working on the lily pads, as he ambled from the depths of the marsh, pushing aside cattails and more. He paused, lifted his head, and scanned the terrain in front of him, but his size gave him a false assurance that there was nothing that could do him harm. He dropped his nose into the water to grab another mouthful and lifted his head as he took a few more steps, moving toward the scattered willows.

Reuben dropped to one knee, lifted his Sharps, and brought the hammer to full cock. Taking a quick sight through the rear ladder and lining the front blade, he waited until the big bull turned his head and with a slow pull, Reuben dropped the hammer. The Sharps roared, driving the butt against Reuben's shoulder, and rocking him back as smoke and fire spat from the muzzle. The bullet flew true and took the bull just behind the big floppy ear, smashing through the neck muscle and splitting the neck bones. The bull dropped to his belly as if he had been poleaxed, his legs splayed out in front of him, his chin on the wet grasses. A grunt emanated that moaned across the river and the marsh as the last of the bull's breath escaped.

Reuben slowly stood, mindlessly reloading the Sharps yet keeping his eyes on the bull. He lifted the lever to cut the paper cartridge and close the breech. Slipping a cap from his possibles pouch, he placed it on the nipple and lowered the hammer to half-cock. He looked back to see Elly nodding and grinning. "Now the work begins," he mumbled. He turned back to the horses, knowing he would need Blue and maybe the pack-mule to get the carcass across the river. He stripped the gear from the mule, tightened the girth on Blue and started to step aboard, but movement at the edge of the trees stopped him.

He casually replaced the Sharps in the scabbard but removed the Henry. He whispered to Elly, "Stay ready, the Arapaho are back." He stepped away from Blue, went to Elly's side and with their rifles across their chests, Reuben spoke loudly in the tongue of the Arapaho, "Ho! My friends, the Arapaho, come and share in my kill. There is more than we need. But you have to help butcher the bull!"

No one moved nor spoke. Reuben whispered to Elly, "They're prob'ly surprised to hear me speak in their tongue."

"Who is this that speaks with the tongue of the *Hinono'eino?*"

"I am Man with Blue Horse, and my woman is Yellow Bird. We are friends of Little Raven."

"I am Little Raven! I do not know you!" said the leader of the hunting party, stepping through the brush with two men slightly behind him. The leader was a young man, Reuben guessed to be about twenty summers, and was an impressive figure. He stood just shy of six feet, broad shouldered with long braids that hung over his broad and deep chest. With a bone hair pipe breast plate, a wide band of silver above his left bicep, a multi-layered bone hair pipe choker and a scalp lock that stood at the back of his head and brandished two feathers. A breech cloth hung below his belt and fringed buckskin leggings topped tall moccasins.

Reuben looked at the man, gave him time to come closer, and responded, "No, you are not the Little Raven we know. You must be his son who uses the same name."

"How do you know my father?"

"We lived with your people a short while when they were on the buffalo hunt up north. Your father and Red Bear, Running Antelope, and Wind in her Hair, tended to my woman and me for our joining ceremony led by your father. We stayed in the lodge for one week, and your mother gave Yellow Bird her horse," he nodded to the horses behind them, "the spotted one."

Little Raven leaned to the side to better see the horses and looked back at Elly, "That was my mother's favorite buffalo hunter. It was a special gift." He frowned, squinted his eyes, and walked a little closer to Elly, looking her up and down, noting especially the rifle cradled in her arms with her finger on the trigger. He nodded his head slowly as if offering his approval and stepped back in front of Reuben. "You said for us to come share your meat. Where?"

Reuben turned to the side, pointed across the river to the carcass of the moose, "There."

Little Raven looked as did his men and one of the men shouted, "Aiiieeee! *Hinenihii!*"

Reuben grinned, "Let your men tend the meat. We

75

will take one," holding up one hand, "backstrap. You and your people can have the rest. My woman will fix some coffee for us while they work."

Little Raven grinned, turned to his men, and gave the directions for them and the others to butcher the moose and sent them on their way. He turned back to Reuben and pointed with his chin to a log beside what would become the fire, and said, "We will wait there."

Reuben chuckled, looked at Elly and said, "I'll get us some firewood while you get the coffee."

Elly shook her head, smiling, knowing the way of the people expected the women to do all the work in preparing the fire and the meal, but she was glad Reuben would at least ready the fire. Yet she also knew he would help her with anything he could to make the visit with the Arapaho hunting party beneficial.

———

WITH AN EARLY START, THEY WERE WELL ON THEIR WAY TO the village of Little Raven's Arapaho band. What started as a clear day with warm sunshine and blue sky, soon began to cloud up in the northwest. Thick dark clouds rolled in and lowered a skirt of darkness. Jagged bolts of lightning lanced the shadows and the rumble of distant thunder seemed to vibrate across the plains. Reuben and Elly rode three abreast with Little Raven while his two close companions sided the mule and followed close behind. Reuben was in the middle with Elly to his right and Little Raven on his left. The two men talked intermittently, but both men warily watched the distant storm.

Reuben nodded to the storm, feeling the cool breeze

on his face, "That appears to be moving south, not too much this way."

Little Raven pointed before them with pursed lips, "The *nisice,* pronghorn, are not concerned. They still graze." He also nodded toward a distant herd with thirty or more animals, about three hundred yards away, that grazed on the lee side of a slight knoll.

"Do your people want some pronghorn meat?" asked Reuben, glancing from the animals to Little Raven.

"They are too far and too fast. If we go toward them, they will be gone before we can take any."

"If you want a couple, I'll shoot them, and your men can dress them out while we continue on to the village."

Little Raven frowned, scowled at Reuben, "You cannot kill one from this far!" and shook his head as he mumbled something about the 'stupid white man.'

Reuben chuckled, reined up, nodded to Elly to stop as well, and stepped down, Sharps and scope in hand. As he stood beside Blue, the hunting party stopped, watching him attach the scope and adjust it. Reuben looked around for any rise in the land, saw a slight lift beside a big sage and slowly walked to the bush. Elly followed close behind as did Bear. When he stopped beside the bush, Elly stepped close and slightly in front and put her fingers in her ears as Reuben lay the fore-stock on her shoulder. He took a few moments to adjust the scope and his sight picture, then whispered to Elly, "Here goes."

Elly unintentionally scrunched up her shoulders, placed her palms flat over her ears and took a deep breath and held it. When Reuben felt her still, he brought the hammer to full cock, checked his sight picture, and slowly squeezed the thin front trigger. The hammer dropped, the cap fired, and the big rifle roared. Smoke spat out the muzzle and the big gun bucked and bounced slightly on Elly's shoulder. She had closed her eyes and now squinted because of the smoke yet watched as a big buck that stood at the edge of the herd, crumpled to the ground. Reuben quickly reloaded, lay the rifle on her shoulder again and repeated the action to drop another buck. The first shot was a distant curiosity to the herd, but the second shot spooked them and within seconds, the entire herd of twenty or thirty had disappeared beyond the tall sage and into one of the swales beyond a rise.

Reuben lowered the rifle, dropped the lever to open the breach and with a small rag wiped the breech clean, inserted another paper cartridge, closed the breach, and replaced the rifle in the scabbard, all while the entire war party watched in silence, a few shaking their heads. When he swung back aboard Blue, the chatter began as Little Raven called for four warriors and sent them after the downed antelope.

The rest of the journey was a little quieter, but it was evident many of the warriors were in awe and envious of the white man with the rifle that could shoot so far and so accurately. Reuben glanced at a grinning Elly, and she shook her head, knowing her man was reveling in the respect of the warriors, yet they both knew any one of the warriors would willingly do whatever they could to take the rifle and more from the white man. With such a weapon, they would be a great warrior, envied by all others.

The village showed in the distance, the many hide lodges almost hidden in the swale. Reuben guessed there to be at least eighty and probably more, that stood as pinnacles of buff and dusty white, the skinny poles protruding above the smoke holes and clawing at the sky. The storm had passed to the west and offered no water for the thirsty desert. The little stream of the Big Sandy or Sand Creek was barely enough for a village of this size, but the people prevailed.

12 / VILLAGE

As they neared the village, children ran to their lodges, women stood to watch as their men returned, and the picture of family life on the plains was painted before them. The horse herd grazed just east of the village, on the far side of the willow shrouded creek. Young men rode around the herd, others sitting horseback and keeping watch. When the hunting party returned, they were warmly greeted and as they passed out the portions of the meat to the different women, there was joy on the faces of everyone, yet some looked at the visitors with suspicion and wonder.

Little Raven led his visitors into the midst of the village, making his way to one of the central lodges and Reuben recognized the layout of the village with the lodges of the leaders situated around the central clearing. As they neared, the word had already spread and Little Raven and his woman, Red Bear, came from the lodge to stand together watching the arrival of the visitors. Red Bear turned to her man, "It is Yellow Bird and her Man with the Blue Horse," she said, smiling and glancing to the visitors. Little Raven nodded, folding his arms across his chest to give the appearance of the dignified and stoic leader of the people.

Reuben lifted his hand to shoulder level, nodding to Little Raven, "It is good to see our friend, Little Raven, and his woman, Red Bear."

Little Raven, maintaining his stoic expression, answered, "It is good to see Man with Blue Horse and his woman, Yellow Bird," answered the chief, motioning for the two to step down.

As Elly touched the ground, Red Bird and Wind in her Hair came to her side and the three women began chattering and led her away. Little Raven motioned to a nearby man who took the horses and mule and led them away. Little Raven turned to his willow back rest that sat just outside the entry to his lodge and motioned for Reuben to join him. It was the custom of the people to sit near the cookfire and talk and with a wave to another back rest, Little Raven and Reuben seated themselves.

Little Raven looked at Reuben, "What brings you to our camp?"

Reuben let a slight grin tug at the corners of his mouth, then looked to the chief, "I heard my friend, and his people were camped here, and we were near, so..." and shrugged.

The chief grinned, nodded, and relaxed his demeanor, "I see your woman still has her spotted horse and my son tells me you have your far shooting rifle."

"Same as we had when we were with you at your buffalo hunt."

"He also said you shared your kill with our people."

"Is that not the way of your people?" asked Reuben, tossing a little stick in the cookfire.

"Ummm," grunted the chief, looking to the sun that was high overhead. He saw Red Bear come from the lodge, followed by Wind in her Hair and Yellow Bird, or Elly, and watched as they sat about preparing the midday meal. Reuben grinned as he watched Elly busy with the others and doing her share of the work.

As the women were busy, Reuben looked to the chief, "Does the chief of the Arapaho still want peace?"

Little Raven looked at Reuben, giving his words considerable thought and wondering what his friend was seeking, then answered, "I have always sought peace with the whites. From the time of the treaty at Fort Laramie, to our visit with the gold seekers, and my journey to see the white chief in the east, and even now after they have once again taken our lands from us, I want peace between our people. Many of our chiefs, of the *Heévâhetaneo'o* or Cheyenne and our people, the *Hinono'eino* or Arapaho, have spoken with the whites, made treaties, but the whites do not honor the words on paper. The soldiers come against us and kill our people. It is hard to make peace with those who only want to destroy our people."

Reuben dropped his eyes to the fire, remaining silent for a few moments, and quietly answered, "Sometimes those things that are most difficult are the most important. If there is no peace, there will be no future for your people. Your women will wail in sorrow for their children and their men, and lodges will be empty."

"The women wail when their children are hungry. When our men are kept from the land of the buffalo and we cannot hunt, our people cannot eat grass like the buffalo. The land where we once hunted the great buffalo, but now I see our women chasing the *beescenee* and *cenee*, the turkey and sage hen, they set snares for *nooku,* the rabbit, and our hunting parties come back with skinny *bih'ih* deer and some have had to eat their horses. It is no way for our people to live."

"So, will you quit trying for peace? Make war instead?" asked Reuben.

"Our young warriors do that, even the one who takes my name, my son, he has led war parties against the whites that come onto our lands and take our game. His warriors have been blooded by war and they want more. When they take the white man's horses and his cows, our people can ride and eat. Would you have them go hungry?"

Reuben shook his head and looked at Little Raven, "I can see your heart is not in this making of war. You have always been a man of peace. You made peace with the Kiowa and Comanche! Even I cannot make peace with the Comanche!" he spat, shaking his head at the memory of his recent fight with the Comanche. "And you have talked of peace with other chiefs and with the white man chiefs, will you not do so again?"

Little Raven twisted in his seat, leaning forward with arms on his knees, "I will seek peace as long as I draw breath. I will leave soon to join Black Kettle and other leaders of the people. The chief of the Cheyenne has called for a council of peace, and I will go to have my say as well."

The women had finished their preparations and began to serve the men. As Little Raven accepted his wooden platter heaped with food, he nodded to Reuben, "That is meat from your kill. We are grateful."

Reuben nodded, grinned, "We are grateful to the Creator who sent the moose to where we could take him."

Little Raven nodded, as if agreeing with Reuben and

watched as Elly came to his side and lay her hand on his shoulder as Reuben spoke a quiet prayer of thanksgiving to the Creator of whom he spoke, and as he closed, he asked God for special strength for the Arapaho people and for wisdom for Little Raven. As he finished with his 'Amen' Little Raven frowned and asked, "You speak to your God as if you know him and he hears you. Can this be so?"

Reuben nodded, accepted the trencher of food from Elly and looked at the chief, "It is my belief, and it is told about in the Bible, that we can know God and His Son in a very real way. When we know him, Jesus, as our personal savior, we are assured of our place in Heaven."

"I would like to know more of this God," began the chief, but before Reuben could answer, he added, "But now is the time for eating."

Reuben grinned and took a good helping of the moose-meat stew and savored the excellent meal. Elly filled her plate and sat beside her husband as did the two women of Little Raven.

Elly looked at Red Bear and asked, "Does your son have a family?"

"No, he has not taken a woman of our people. He believes he must fight against the whites. His war party had taken a captive white woman, but another man took her for his woman. Little Raven, our son, has told his men they were not to take captives or fight the women, but each man does as he wants. That is the way of our people, one cannot tell another what he can or cannot do, especially in times of war."

"Does that woman live here in the village?" asked Elly, trying to show a calm demeanor but Reuben knew she was upset at the thought of a captive woman here.

"No, the warrior who took her was a Cheyenne. He has returned to his village with Bull Bear, the dog soldiers."

Little Raven could see Elly's emotion was more than curiosity and he joined, "We are going to meet with other chiefs soon to talk peace with the white man. Black Kettle wants to buy or trade for all white captives and trade them back to the white soldiers to show our intention for peace is real."

Elly slowly lifted her head and looked at the chief, knowing him to be a man of peace, and believed the woman would soon be freed. Her shoulders sagged in an obvious show of relief as she looked to her food and began to eat. Wind in her Hair and Red Bear looked to one another, a silent thought passing between them and understanding the concerns of their friend, Yellow Bird.

Reuben looked to Little Raven, "Did all your hunting parties return with game?"

Little Raven let a bit of a grin split his face, understanding what Reuben was doing by changing the subject of their discussion, then with a slight nod, "Yes, but some had very little. All had deer, some turkey, but none had moose or antelope."

Reuben smiled, "But they will go out again soon?"

"Yes. But some, like our son, have left to raid the wagons and ranches of the white men. They have found greater bounty when they raid than when they hunt."

Reuben could offer no argument for what Little Raven said, for it was true that the bounty from white men was greater. When their hunting lands had continually been taken from them, they had been offered rations and trade goods, but the rations and trade goods never came or if they did, it was not in the amounts promised.

Reuben knew it was a natural thing for a man to do whatever he could to feed his family and his people. He could not fault them for that, for under the same circumstances, he would probably do the same.

13 / TRUST

Bear lay beside Elly. The faint shadow crossed between the loose blanket that covered the opening to the lodge where they were sleeping and brought Bear's head up, a low growl stirring both Reuben and Elly. She put her hand on the dog's scruff, whispered, "Shhh boy, we hear him." She felt Reuben slip his Bowie knife from under his folded coat he used as a pillow and through slitted eyes saw her man turn to face the entry. She lay on her side facing Reuben, Bear behind her, and they saw the shadowy figure push through the entry and pause in a crouch just inside the lodge. Moonlight pierced the smoke hole, the lance of light catching the thin trail of smoke that whispered up from the embers of the central fire.

With the dim light showing the intruder's face, he was not a familiar figure to Reuben, but his youthful features mottled with perspiration glistened as he moved. The young man began to rifle through the packs that lay near the entry, searching for something special as he pushed things aside. His attention focused on his search, he did not see Reuben move, but the sleeping

87

figure of the white man lifted from the blankets, grabbed the one braid that hung down the man's back and jerked him to the ground. Wide eyes stared up as he muttered his surprise but the knife at his throat and the man that had suddenly straddled his body made him catch his breath and try to bring his arms up to defend himself, but the knees of the white man held his arms to his side.

Bear had come to his feet, bounding over Elly, and growling and snapping within inches of the intruder's face. Wide eyes, open mouth that could not make a sound, and fear made the young man tremble, thinking he was moments from death. But the low voice of Reuben asked in the tongue of the people, "Why do you come into my lodge uninvited?"

The young man gasped for air, looking from the open maw of the big dog that resembled a black bear, and into the face of the big white man whose weight on his middle made it difficult to breathe. He muttered, "The far shooting rifle – I wanted it to be a great warrior!" he answered, keeping his voice low.

"A dead warrior is not a great warrior. Your people will sing songs about you and how stupid you were to try to steal from a friend of the people!"

The young man tried to squirm from under the weight but could not move, yet he knew the people would only sing songs about him if he had crossed over and no longer walked among his people.

"What is your name?" asked Reuben, keeping the blade pressing flat against the intruder's throat.

"*To'uubexookee* Bobcat."

"You were about to be a dead bobcat!" stated Reuben, rising from the young man, and motioning him to sit up. "It is not the weapon that makes a great warrior, it is his bravery and honor. That can be shown with any weapon or with no weapon. Is it not a great thing to count coup?"

The young man nodded, touching his throat to see if there was blood. He looked up to Reuben, waiting.

"When a warrior counts coup, it is great bravery to touch an enemy without killing him, is that right?"

The young man, still nervous and continually looking around, watching the man and his woman but especially the big wolf-like dog who continually snarled at the young man.

Reuben reached for his buckskin jacket, jerked a couple long pieces of the fringe from the sleeve and held it out to the young man. "Take this, tell your friends you counted coup on the Man with the Blue Horse. I will not deny that."

The young man tentatively accepted the fringe, looking up at the strange white man, and down at the fringe in his hand.

"Now go, before I decide to take your scalp!" demanded Reuben, making a gruff face.

The young man jumped to his feet and lunged through the opening, almost tearing the hanging blanket from the doorway, and disappeared into the darkness. Reuben chuckled, looked at Elly who was smiling broadly and they both laughed together. When Bear came to her side, she motioned for him to lay down and she lay back, pulling the blanket up to her neck as she watched Reuben adjust the entry blanket, and slip his Bowie back into the scabbard. He lay beside her, shaking his head slightly, mumbling, "Kid's got guts, but if he doesn't change a mite, those guts'll be spread all over the desert!"

Elly curled up beside her man, put her hand on his chest, "What you did was a good thing. He will gain honor among his friends, and he will see you as a friend."

"If he lives long enough," mumbled Reuben, placing his hand over hers and turning to face her. The moonlight illumined their smiles as they looked at one another, and as was their habit, they savored the moment of closeness, before dropping off to sleep.

———

CHIEF LITTLE RAVEN CAME TO THEIR MORNING COOKFIRE and at Reuben's invitation, joined him on the blanket nearby. The chief glanced toward Elly who was busy making some cornmeal biscuits for the Dutch Oven, and back to Reuben. "I will go today to join Black Kettle and the other chiefs. We will talk of peace with the whites."

"Will there be many leaders there?" asked Reuben.

"Yes. Many leaders from the Cheyenne and other leaders of the Arapaho. The Sioux, Comanche, and Kiowa have also been bidden."

"I hope you will be able to hash out a good agreement and soon. William Bent told me he was going to see Black Kettle so he might be there also."

"His son, *Ho-my-ike*, is the son of Owl Woman, the daughter of White Thunder, a Cheyenne chief. He will be there to translate and speak."

Reuben was silent for a moment, looked up at Little Raven, "Your son is raiding the ranches and stages north of here. We will go to the Smoky Hill stage road and stations to help the stage company get through safely. If your son and his warriors come against us, I will not hold fire," cautioned Reuben.

"I have told him this, but he leads a band of young and eager warriors who seek honors, bounty and goods for their people and to buy women for their lodges. It is against our ways to try to tell another what they cannot do when they bring food to the people."

"I understand, Little Raven. But I must also protect my people."

Little Raven looked long at Reuben, thinking, and quietly rose to his feet as did Reuben. The two men faced one another as Little Raven extended his hand and the two friends clasped forearms, putting their free hand on the other's shoulder, "You are a friend, and you must do as you will. I too, must do what is best for my people. We will meet again, and we will be friends," declared Little Raven.

"Indeed," answered Reuben, watching as Little Raven turned away to go to his lodge and prepare for his journey.

Reuben looked at Elly, shaking his head, "I sure hope we never have to go against him in battle."

Elly looked at her man and at the back of Little Raven as he picked his way back to his lodge. She knew the men were friends and neither would want to shed the blood of the other, nor the blood of any of his people.

———

THE SMOKY HILL TRAIL STRETCHED ACROSS THE MILES OF bunch grass, cacti, and sagebrush like a thin pale line winding its way as it traced the low water river. Patches of green showed at the snake bends of the river where cottonwoods lifted scraggly branches, many grey with death, and a few that tenuously clung to the fluttering leaves. Below the tall snags clustered alders, willows, and a few chokecherry bushes. A flat-topped sod hut stood beside a corral fashioned with crooked limbs. One man sat on a crude bench, soaking up the mid-day sun, his floppy hat covering his eyes as he leaned against the sod walls.

The steady shuffle of two horses and a pack-mule foretold the arrival of two visitors to the lone hut and the man pushed up the brim of his hat, squinted against the bright sun and spat a black stream of overused tobacco juice. A small trickle found its way through the familiar path of the man's chin whiskers, and he wiped his ragged sleeve across his beard to absorb the dribbles. A voice resembling the hoarse croak of a turkey buzzard called, "Howdy folks!"

Reuben reined up and leaned forward, his forearm on the pommel of his saddle as he pushed his hat back and answered, "Howdy!" He chuckled a moment, looking around the lonesome place and asked, "This here the Smoky River Trail?"

"Wal, since yonder's the Smoky Hill River, an' this's the onliest trail aroun', I reckon it is!" answered the grizzly old man. The whiskers that were not stained by tobacco juice showed grey that matched the friar's ring that rested on his ears. Once his hat was pushed back from his eyes, a sunburned pate showed to be hairless above the friar's ring. A quick glance showed as many stains on the ragtag shirt and britches as were on his whiskers and when the wind shifted, it was obvious the man stayed shy of the river.

"Had many wagons by lately?" asked Reuben.

"Oh, this mornin' they was a dozen freighters makin' fer the gold fields. They was follered by eight or ten wagons o' settlers or gold hunters."

"Any Indians about?"

The old man frowned, shaking his head as he looked at Reuben like he was looking at a greenhorn, "Course they is! Ain't they allus aroun'? Why, there be Cheyenne, 'Rapaho, Sioux, and who knows what all. They come 'roun' wantin' ta trade, but I ain't got nuthin' they want. If they's lookin' fer trouble," he patted a rifle beside him that Reuben recognized as a Colt revolving shotgun. "They buried a few out yonder, so they shucks shy o' ol' man Colt!"

"That's smart," answered Reuben. He nodded toward the river, "Ain't this the area they call Cheyenne Wells?'

"Ummhmmm, cuz them Cheyenne claim some springs wut feeds the crick yonder. If you'ns stickin' 'roun', there's a fair ta' middlin' campsite down yonder at the bend in the river."

"We just might do that," replied Reuben, lifting the reins on Blue, and nudging him to the side of the old man's sod hut. He tipped his hat as they left and pointed to the river. As Elly came alongside, he spoke softly, "This'll give us a camp near where the chiefs are meeting and maybe give us a lead on the wagons and such. But for now, I'm lookin' for some coffee!'

"And I'm lookin' for some fresh air!" shared Elly, fanning the air before her face as if to rid the area of the stench of the unwashed hut dweller.

93

14 / TRAVELERS

"It still amazes me that the governor thinks the two of us can do anything about the Indians and the raiding and such. He's got the entire First and Third Colorado Cavalry and their misguided leader, Chivington, and he has the Colorado Rangers, all to do his bidding to, what was it he said, *'To go in pursuit of all hostile Indians on the plains... to kill and destroy, as enemies of the country, wherever they may be found...'* and he expects the two of us to do what?"

Reuben chuckled at the oft repeated remarks of his woman, shaking his head, "If you remember, he and Chivington both are wannabe politicians, and to get where they want, which is in congress in Washington, they're covering all bases. They don't want any voter asking, 'why didn't you use the U.S. Marshals?' or whoever else they might think of or imagine." He paused a moment, shaking his head and reached for the coffee to pour himself a cup. Looking back at Elly he continued, "Most of the boys in blue aren't too enthusiastic about chasing the Indians, and the Colorado Rangers are usually kept in or near Denver City to help the city police, so none of 'em have been too successful at stopping the Indian attacks. Maybe if the agencies would pay the annuities and rations like the treaties promised, that would also help keep them on the reservations."

Elly set the coffee pot back on the big rock beside the small fire, leaned back and looked at Reuben, "As far as I'm concerned, I've had enough of this marshal stuff. After we get done with this, whatever 'this' is, I'm all for turning in these badges and hightail it outta here and avoid telegraph offices for the rest of our days!"

Reuben chuckled, "I thought you liked bein' the only woman marshal!"

"Nosireebob! Not a day of it! I only took the badge cuz you did!" she declared, shaking her head, and tossing a stick on the fire. She had already prepared a Dutch Oven full of biscuits that sat on some coals and with more coals on the lid at the edge of the fire. The biscuits would add to the last of the moose meat and potatoes, onions, and cattail shoots that would be fixed in the frying pan for their supper.

She looked over at her man, shook her head and frowned, "If we don't go back to the cabin 'fore winter, you thinkin' about someplace else?"

He grinned, reached for her to draw her closer to him and said, "Maybe north to the high country, or south to Santa Fe."

Their quiet moments were interrupted by the crack of a whip, the clarion sound of a messenger's bugle, and the rattle of trace chains that signaled the arrival of a stage coming from the east. They knew the sod hut and the corral with eight mules told of the hut being a way station for a stage line and had expected a stage to come through anytime.

"There's the stage you were expecting!" stated Elly,

standing, and turning to look at the trail to see the Concord coach rock to a stop before the hut. "That's not one of Holladay's coaches, is it?"

"Nah, the way I understand it is that's a small company called the Western Stage line. It has yet to land any lucrative mail contracts but been making its way with the many gold seekers and others that are coming because of the gold strike, usually to mine gold from the miners instead of the ground." He chuckled at the image of so many places throughout South Park and other gold strikes that had sprung up to relieve the prospectors of their newfound riches. "The Smoky Hill trail is considered a short cut and more direct route to the gold fields than either the Cherokee trail or the Overland Trail, but it also has its problems. Some call it 'Starvation Trail' cuz of the story of the Blue brothers that resorted to cannibalism just to make it across the flatlands where there was no water. It's also the most susceptible to Indian attacks, being so far from any of the army forts or any towns."

Elly frowned at the mention of cannibalism, making a contorted face to show her contempt for such an action. "Cannibalism, really?"

"Ummhmm, I'm sure there's more of it than most know. I heard tell it tastes just like chicken!" declared a grinning Reuben.

Elly grinned, "The only thing that tastes like chicken is chicken! Don't give me that!" she declared, throwing a little stick at him playfully.

He ducked the stick, "I think I'm goin' over to talk to the driver and shotgunner, see what they might have seen along the trail." He turned away and started for the horses to saddle Blue. He had no sooner turned his back than a sudden barrage of gunfire came from near the station that made Reuben turn back, rifle in hand.

Elly glanced back at her man, "Looks like Little Raven and his war party!" she declared, running to the stack of gear to grab her rifle. Their camp was more than a hundred yards from the station, and the flats offered little cover other than clumps of sage or rabbit brush, neither able to do anything but obscure and not protect.

Reuben stood beside a tall cottonwood, watching the band converge on the station from two sides. The hostler and others had crammed into the little sod hut and fired from the doorway and single window. The sides and rear of the hut had no openings which also made the occupants blind to any attack from the rear. Reuben made a quick survey of the terrain between them and the hut and made an estimate of the number of attackers to be about twenty. He turned to Elly, "We've got to help them, but..." he turned and ran back to the gear, swapping his Henry for the Sharps. He always kept all his weapons loaded, but not with the cap in place, and now as he moved back to the tree, he brought the hammer back to half-cock and placed a cap on the nipple.

He glanced at Elly, "Don't fire unless they come after us, then just keep them off me while I try to whittle 'em down a little!" She nodded and took up a position near another big cottonwood, leaning against it and using it as a leaning rest, watching the attackers and waiting.

The attackers had split into two groups, one continuing its frontal assault on the hut, the other swinging wide and coming between the hut and the campsite by the river. Reuben brought the Sharps to bear on one of the leaders who had led the others to go to ground, leaving their horses near the trees. When the man raised up to motion to his warriors, Reuben dropped the hammer. The Sharps bucked and did its job, the warrior took the slug high on his chest, just below his throat. The man grabbed at his shattered bone hair pipe breast plate, eyes flaring. He tried to lift his hand and shout but spat blood and crumpled to his knees.

The rapid rattle of gunfire from both the attackers and defenders masked the roar of the Sharps, but it still brought the attention of some of the warriors away from the hut and to the trees. As Reuben reloaded, he watched the attackers, some looking back toward the river and their location. He waited, watching and when it appeared none were looking his direction, he saw one rise up to approach the hut, and Reuben quickly brought the sight to bear and squeezed off the shot. The man stumbled and fell, prompting another to look back at the trees to try to spot the shooter, but he did not live long enough to tell the others.

As he reloaded, Reuben saw several scampering about, but instead of going toward the hut, they were moving from sage to sage, working their way toward him. "They're coming our way! If you get a clear shot, take it, but move to another position quickly!" he called to Elly. He saw her nod and lift her rifle. Before he could pick another target, he heard the bark of the Henry and saw an attacker stumble and fall. The sound of Elly jacking another round into the chamber told Reuben she was also on the move, and he watched for another target, spotted a man rise from one clump of sage and Reuben kept his eyes and sight on the clump, waiting for movement. As the man came to a crouch readying to move closer, the big .52 caliber slug from the Sharps split the sage and knocked him to his back. Again, the Henry barked, and another attacker fell.

As Reuben brought the Sharps up again, movement to the side betrayed the attack of four warriors trying to flank them. "Four coming to your right!" he shouted, as he drew a bead on one. The Sharps bucked and one attacker stumbled, but the other three were nearing the tree line. Elly fired, spinning one around before he fell to his face, still holding his shoulder. The other two hesitated, until Reuben fired the Sharps just before dropping it and drawing his Remington pistol on the run. He ran towards her as she jacked another round into the Henry and lifted it to her shoulder, but the sole remaining warrior was charging and knocked the Henry aside with his war club and reared it back above his head to bring it down, but Reuben's Remington roared, and the man's arm splintered as the .44 slug struck his elbow. The warrior grabbed his elbow as he turned toward the charging Reuben. The warrior spun, grabbed at Elly with his good arm, but she had brought her Colt around, cocking the hammer as she did and dropped the hammer as the muzzle pushed against the man's belly. The Colt's muffled blast drove the man back, his flesh burned with the powder and the slug tearing through his middle to blow a hole through his back, taking part of his spine with it. The warrior appeared to melt into the ground as he crumpled in death, Elly stepping back away and watching him die as she cocked the hammer over another bullet, ready if needed.

Reuben came to her side, looking at her and at the downed warrior. He turned to search the field between them and the station, saw two others running back to their horses and swing aboard, driving the dead men's horses before them and shouting at the other warriors.

Within moments, all had disappeared over the slight rise beyond the station. The stench of gunsmoke and death hung heavy in the air as Reuben and Elly walked back to their horses. He finished rigging Blue, saddled Daisy for Elly and they both swung aboard to go check on the people at the station.

15 / WAGONS

As Reuben and Elly neared the station, he called out to those inside, "Hey inside! We're comin' 'round front! Don't shoot! The Indians have all gone!" He paused, heard the rumblings of talk inside the small hut, and nudged Blue to move around toward the front of the station. The door had been opened and the shutters on the windows were pushed out as the men began to come out, weapons in hand, looking around cautiously. Those behind the first men pushed their way past, gasping for air and coughing and spitting. As the group exited the station, Reuben swung down, nodded to Elly to also step down and as she did, he noticed a hand carved sign that appeared to have been the butt stock of a rifle. He frowned as he tried to make out the words, *Dog Hose*, he formed the words and looked at Elly and back at the sign as she said, "I think it's 'posed to say *Dog House*."

Reuben frowned and looked back at his woman, then saw the hostler come from the hut and he asked, "What's that sign about?" pointing to the stock over the door.

The whiskery old man chuckled, "What'chu think? It say Dog House, that's cuz the Injuns said I was like a

101

prairie dog, whut with livin' in a soddy. They thot it were like them prairie dogs that make their home underground."

Elly, standing slightly behind Reuben, whispered, "Smells like one, too!"

Reuben chuckled and looked at the other men, the Jehu, or driver of the stage, the shotgunner, also called messenger, and five passengers, all men. One was dressed like a peddler, the others roughly attired and probably headed for the gold fields. The peddler was bent over, breathing heavily and coughing. He stood up and looked at one of the other men, "So help me, I don't know which was worse, the Indians outside or that stinkin' ol' man on the inside! What with the powder smoke and his stench, I thought I was gonna die without getting shot."

The other man nodded, glancing at the hostler and back to the peddler, "I thought about shootin' him, but I figgered he'd smell worse dead than alive! And there was no tellin' how long we'd be locked up in there with him!"

A third man chimed in, "I'm s'prised that sign don't say *Skunk House!*"

Another passenger called out to the Jehu, "When we gonna get outta here?"

"Oh, don't go gettin' riled! We don't know where them Injuns went an' they might be waitin' fer us further on!" answered the driver.

"Maybe that wagon comin' will have some news for us," suggested Reuben as he shaded his eyes to look to the west. At first, it appeared to be a lone wagon, but as the dust cloud was blown aside, the canvas tops of four wagons could be seen. As the wagons approached, the men and Elly stood near the station, waiting, and watching as the small train pulled up near the station.

Reuben took in the sight as the wagons drew up, noting each was pulled by a four up of horses and three wagons also had saddled horses trailing behind. Two men sat on the seat of the first wagon, and it appeared that each wagon had at least two men and there were no women or children to be seen.

Reuben stepped forward and greeted the men, "Howdy folks. Been on the trail long?"

"Howdy!" answered the driver of the first wagon. "We're comin' from South Park, headin' home!" he declared with a broad grin.

"See any Indians?" asked Reuben, watching the men climb down to stretch their legs as they looked around for an outhouse. When one of the stage passengers motioned to the back of the station, one of the men made haste to get there.

"Nah, nary a one! You?" asked the driver.

"We had a bit of a set to with a war party of Arapaho renegades just a little bit ago," replied Reuben. "The stage driver," nodding to the Jehu, "was wonderin' how the road was and if there were any hostiles."

"Road ain't much, but ain't seen no Injuns!" answered the driver, nodding toward the back of the station and the outhouse. The first man returned, and the driver of the wagon hot footed it to the back house.

"Did I hear right? You had a fight with some Indians?" asked the returnee.

Reuben chuckled, "You heard right. There were about twenty at the start, but we whittled 'em down a mite and the rest hightailed it."

"What kind was they?" asked the man.

"Arapaho, most of 'em, anyway." He pointed to the sage on the far side of the road and explained, "There's a few of 'em yonder," and nodded behind the station, "and

103

some more back there. Don't expect 'em to be there long cuz they usually come back after their dead."

"Then maybe we better get a move on!" declared the man as he started to the other wagons to report the news.

One of the other men came to the group in front of the station and asked, "So, how's the road thataway?" nodding to the east.

The driver spoke up, "It's alright, nuthin' to write home about, but it'll do. So, what's the news from back yonder," nodding to the west.

The man chuckled, "Wal, Chivington declared martial law in Denver City, ain't lettin' nobody outta town. That was the last straw fer us. We was plannin' on goin' home anyhow, but when that happened, and the word came that the Platte River road was closed cuz o' Injuns, and they was talkin' 'bout closin' the others, we figgered we better skedaddle! All of us did alright in the goldfields, got us a stake fer our families, so we figgered it'd be better to leave now 'stead o' gettin' greedy and stayin' on too long."

"Any news about the war?" asked one of the passengers.

"Ain't heard nuthin' new. Onliest thing folks talkin' 'bout is the Injun wars."

Reuben looked sternly at the man, "And yet you and these others think you can make it through?"

The man shook his head, glancing up at the men standing by the wagons, "We got us fourteen well-armed men, most experienced with the war, and we figger it ain't no worse on the trail than it is in the gold fields. If we're gonna cash in our chips, might as well be tryin' to get home in the doin' of it."

Reuben extended his hand to shake with the man, "Then good luck to you!" he declared.

The man nodded, shaking Reuben's hand, "It wouldn't hurt, if you're a prayin' man, to put in a good word for us!"

"We'll do that!" answered Reuben, Elly standing beside him and nodding her agreement.

They watched as the men mounted the wagons and pulled out, waving as they passed and disappearing over the slight rise to the east. The hostler had been busy with the mules for the stage, having already put the first team into the corrals before the attack, he now rigged the six spare mules and backed them into place to hook the trace chains to the single trees. Satisfied, he stepped away and nodded to the Jehu who hollered to the passengers, "Alright, get aboard! We're leavin'!"

————

WHERE JUST A SHORT WHILE AGO, THERE HAD BEEN A GUN battle raging and gunsmoke laying low on the sage, now there was silence. The wagons had passed through, the stage was gone, and Reuben and Elly looked at the station keeper and Reuben asked, "Prairie Dog?"

The whiskery old man chuckled, "Suits me, don't it?"

Reuben chuckled, shaking his head, and looked back at the man, "You expect any more stages soon?"

"Nah, usually one, maybe two on a good day, but won't be none till maybe *mañana*. And if them renegades have anything to say 'bout it, maybe not then!" he shrugged. "But thar's usually wagons galore, ya' know, freighters an' settlers an' such." He paused, stubbed his toe in the dirt, "But, ain't been too many o' them neither."

"I think we might be camped yonder for a day or two,

so don't go gettin' spooked an' start shootin' thataway, y'hear?"

The man cackled, chompin' with his toothless gums, his pointed chin almost touching his nose when he chewed on his tobacco. He spat a stream of dark juice, wiped his face with his sleeve and added, "Ahhh, thet Colt shotgun won't shoot that fer anyhow!" and cackled again.

Reuben shook his head, nodded to Elly and they mounted up and turned back to the campsite by the river. As they crossed the flats where the Arapaho renegades had mounted their attack, they noted the bodies were all gone. Reuben shook his head, "They musta come when we were on the other side of the station. Don't that beat all!"

16 / PASSERSBY

Eight big freighters, heavily laden with foodstuffs, staples, and rifles for the people of Denver City, moved slowly along the Smoky Hill Trail staying just north of Big Sandy Creek. Scouting for the wagons and well ahead of the train, rode Reuben and Elly following close behind Bear, the big black dog that always took the lead. Because of the fear of raiding Indians, the wagonmaster had implored them to scout for the train since they were carrying much needed supplies for the many people that were isolated in Denver City. Colonel Chivington had declared martial law and forbid anyone from leaving and the primary route for traders and freighters was the Overland Trail, or Platte River trail, and it had been closed because of the marauding Indians.

It was pushing close to mid-day when the road mounted a slight rise and dropped over the western slope to come within sight with a band of Indians, numbering close to fifty, who were riding to the south. Without the band showing any sign of aggression, Reuben looked to Elly, "Stay close to the wagons, drop back, and tell them to hold up, but draw close to one another. I'm going to ride ahead, see if I can talk."

"Be careful!" she ordered as she whistled for Bear and reined around to return to the wagons. She knew the Indians were too far away to alarm the wagons, but they needed to be warned and prepared. She kicked Daisy up to a canter and quickly stopped the wagons. As she drew near, she spoke to the wagonmaster, Homer Westlake, "Hold up! Get your other wagons, two abreast and close together, there's a band of Indians up ahead!"

"Where's Reuben?" asked Westlake, frowning.

"He'll try to talk to 'em, but get your wagons close up and ready, just in case!" she repeated, "NOW!" she demanded. The sudden shout spurred the wagonmaster to action and within moments of riding alongside the wagons and shouting his orders, the eight wagons were bunched together, bullwhackers and other teamsters taking position with rifles at the ready.

Reuben rode slowly toward the band that moved in a large group, close together but with room to spare, a common maneuver of the plains people. It was an easily defensible formation, but also one that could quickly be turned into an offensive tactic. As he approached, four warriors broke from the band and charged toward Reuben, screaming war cries and brandishing weapons, but Reuben held his ground, lifting one hand in the sign of peace. The warriors encircled Reuben and pointing to the band, hollered in the tongue of the Arapaho, "Go! Our leader, Little Raven, demands you come!"

Reuben grinned and answered, "Little Raven is my friend. I will be glad to talk with him," nudging his mount forward to join the still moving cavalcade of warriors of both the Arapaho and Cheyenne people.

As Reuben came near, Little Raven recognized his

friend and motioned him closer. "I see we meet again, Man with Blue Horse. Why are you here?"

"We were scouting for some freighters goin' to Denver City, but we also hoped to see you and hear the good news of your council with Black Kettle."

"Ride with me and we will talk," offered Little Raven, looking around, "Where is your woman, Yellow Bird?"

Reuben grinned, nodding, "She is with the freighters and waits for my return."

Little Raven nodded, waited until Reuben was alongside and began, "We had a good council. *Niwot*," he began, motioning to the man who rode beside him, "our peace chief who leads the other band of *Hinono'eino*, War Bonnet, White Antelope, and One Eye of the *Heévâhetaneo'o*, were there and Tall Bull and Bull Bear of the Dog Soldiers. All but Tall Bull want peace, but Tall Bull and the Dog Soldiers left the council." He paused, looking at Reuben, and continued, "We had Bent make a letter to ask the soldiers to make peace with the Arapaho, Cheyenne, Kiowa, Comanche, Apache and Sioux. The letter asks to trade prisoners. Niwot has traded for two women and a child, and the tribes have four more. We will trade these for any of our people held by the soldiers. We want peace and no more war," he declared emphatically.

"That is good, Little Raven. It does my heart good to hear you say that. The letter, will it be given to the soldiers?" queried Reuben.

"One Eye and Eagle Head and One Eye's wife, will take it to Fort Lyon to give to Wynkoop." He looked at Reuben, dropped his eyes and added, "We also told them there were three war parties out, two Arapaho, one Cheyenne, but they are expected back soon."

Reuben nodded, "Yeah, I know. I think it was your

son and his party that attacked the stage station back at Cheyenne Wells. They lost several men in the fight before they left."

"My son?" asked Little Raven.

"I don't think he was hit," answered Reuben, looking at the chief.

Little Raven nodded, and fell silent, slowly shaking his head.

"So, what will you do now?" asked Reuben.

Little Raven looked at his friend and began to explain, "We will return to our village and wait for the answer from One Eye and Eagle Head. They are to bring the soldiers from the fort to a place of council. Our people will meet them and have the council to give up the captives and what the soldiers say will tell us what we as a people will do. If it is to have peace, we will have a council to talk and agree."

"Was Bent with you at the peace council?"

"He was there, and his son was also there. They helped make up the letter for the soldiers. He left the council to return to his home."

"Good. Yellow Bird and I will go to see Bent and we will be close to Fort Lyon so we can hear what happens with the letter." They rode in silence for a few moments until Reuben reined up and extended his hand to Little Raven, "I will leave you now. You know where I will be and if I can be of any help to you, send someone for me."

Little Raven leaned over to grasp forearms with Reuben and added, "I will offer prayers to *Chebbeniathan* and ask that you do the same with your God."

Reuben nodded, "I will definitely do that, my friend."

Reuben reined Blue away from the band and nudged him into a canter to return to the wagons and Elly. He was surprised to see a stage stopped alongside the freight wagons and Elly sitting her horse beside the stage, talking to the shotgunner. He pulled up near them and nodded to the driver, looked at Elly as she asked, "Everything alright?"

"Ummhmm," he answered and looked at the driver and shotgunner as the wagonmaster of the freighters came near, "They were coming from a peace council of the Arapaho, Cheyenne, Dog Soldiers, and some Sioux. They're wantin' to make peace with the soldier boys and us white men, so they made up a letter to take to the fort and start the process."

"You don't say!" declared the wagonmaster. "Now if that don't beat all! I thought all them redskins wanted was to kill white men and take scalps, and now you say they're wantin' peace? I don't believe it!"

"Why not? They're smart folks, and I know some of 'em personally, and know for a fact they've done more for peace than about all the politicians combined! Most of the treaties they've made were broken by the white men!" stated Reuben, his dander up a mite. "Actually, truth be known, this land we're on right now was the land of the Arapaho and Cheyenne, and the treaty of Fort Laramie back in '51 promised it would be theirs forever. But when gold was found, then all the runaways from the war came stormin' through here and killin' the buffalo and Indians and broke the treaty! Then they signed another'n that took away most of the land, and the white men broke it again!" He shook his head, breathing heavy and trying to calm down. The driver, shotgunner, and wagonmaster were staring at him, surprised at his vehemence, then the wagonmaster asked quietly, "Is it alright for us to push on?"

"Yeah, go ahead. We're," motioning to Elly and

himself, "goin' back to Fort Lyon and meet up with William Bent. We got some things to settle."

The wagonmaster started back to his wagons and the driver of the stage uncoiled his whip and shouted at the mules as he cracked the long bull whip over their heads. The wagon rocked back on its traces, the mules dug in their hooves, and as the trace chains rattled the stage started away, putting themselves ahead of the slower moving freighters.

Elly looked at Reuben and said, "If we're goin' back to the fort, you better get the mule behind that freighter yonder!" motioning to the last freighter that appeared to be waiting for them. Reuben nodded, nudging Blue toward the wagon and with a wave to the driver, bent down and slipped the knot from the wagon and pulled their pack mule aside.

17 / RETURN

The wide expanse of the grassland prairie stretched out before them, the Smoky Hill River behind them showed the only green for miles in any direction. Dirty blue sage stood as scattered clumps with shadows beginning to stretch back to the east, faded green of the usually yellow blossomed rabbit brush was heavy with the dry alkaline dust that was carried by the lonesome winds. Elly and Reuben rode side by side, Bear no more than fifty feet before them. Every drop of a hoof raised billows of dust that filtered up from the thin brown buffalo grass. Elly looked at Reuben, "I was talkin' to the stage driver and his messenger, or listening was more like it. They were tellin' about the latest news, seems there was a bunch of Confederate outlaws called the Reynolds gang that was caught by the soldier boys and taken to Denver City." She paused, looking at the wide-eyed surprise that painted Reuben's face.

"Caught by the soldier boys?! That's a bald-faced lie if I ever heard one! You know it was us what caught them rebels and turned 'em over to the soldier boys!" he blubbered, his exasperation showing. "That's just like those

100-day enlistees, can't do nothin' on their own so they have to take credit for what we do!" He shook his head, turning to face his woman, "What else did he say?"

"He said Chivington ordered Captain Cree and some of the 3rd Regiment to escort them boys to Fort Lyon for a military trial, and even though it's a nine-day trip, he wouldn't allow 'em to take any rations!"

Reuben frowned, giving Elly a confused look, and asked, "And?"

"And when the escort got to Russellville, it seems all the prisoners tried to escape, and the soldiers were *forced* to kill 'em all!"

Reuben reined up, frowning, and looked at Elly, "They did what?!"

"You heard me. They killed 'em all! And get this, rumor has it that Chivington was braggin' about ordering their execution!"

Reuben shook his head, grumbled, "And that knot head claimed to be a Methodist Preacher! If that don't beat all!" He nudged Blue to move and glanced at Elly, "Mark my words, that ain't the last we'll hear of that man!"

"Prob'ly not!" agreed Elly.

They rode in silence for a while until Elly asked, "Think we'll get to the fort before the Arapaho with the letter asking for peace?"

"I hope so. I'd like to be there when it comes, but I reckon we'll find out from Bent 'bout that."

———

THEY WERE MOVING IN A SOUTHWEST DIRECTION, BOUND for Fort Lyon, as the sun bore down upon their shoulders and brought sweat to every part of their upper torso, the salty moisture burning the edges of their eyes as they squinted into the distance. Bear had slowed, casting about, and looking behind them until he stopped with head lifted and letting a low growl come from deep in his chest. He glanced to Elly and to Reuben, looking behind them and showing alarm with ears pricked and hackles raised. Reuben stopped, brow wrinkled and twisted around in his saddle. Behind them, at a distance he guessed to be about a mile, dust lifted to show they were pursued by several riders. He glanced to Elly, saw she was also looking at the billowing dust, and looked at him wide-eyed.

Reuben twisted around, looking for any cover, "There! Looks like what might be a creek!" A low line of dark green hinted at juniper and piñon. "Let's go! They already know we're here; they're followin' our tracks!" He slapped legs to Blue and the big gelding lunged forward, the lead of the mule drew tight, but the mule quickly matched the gelding step for step. Elly had kicked Daisy to a canter, keeping pace with Blue, and they headed for the draw.

As they crested the slight rise, the slope dropped into a dry alkaline creek bed, bordered with scrubby piñon and rocks. It was the cover they needed. Quickly dropping from their horses, Elly had her Henry in hand and went to a big rock that had a scraggly piñon doing its best to split the rock with its stubborn roots. She grinned as she thought she had both cover and shade but glanced to Reuben who was rapidly tethering the horses and mule further away, in some thick juniper.

He quickly came to her side, both Sharps and Henry in hand, the case with the binoculars hanging around his neck. He grinned at her, lay his Henry beside her, "I'm goin' up there," nodding to the rise that shielded them from their pursuers, "and see what they're doin', maybe cut down the odds a mite."

"Hurry back! I'm not interested in being left alone to entertain our guests!" she grinned as she jacked a round into the chamber of her Henry.

Reuben nodded, turning away, and taking the slope with his long-legged stride. As he crested the slight knoll, he dropped to his belly and brought out the binoculars. He focused in on the riders, counting about a dozen natives, guessing them to be Comanche or Kiowa returning to the south after a raid. They were driving a small bunch of riderless horses, probably stolen from some rancher. As he watched, he saw the leaders gesticulating and pointing in the direction where he sat, and pointing at the tracks before them, undoubtedly wanting to pursue them and take some more bounty and horses to complete their raid.

Reuben lowered the binoculars, slipped the scope for the Sharps from his belt and began attaching it to the big rifle. He tightened it down as he watched the riders coming. Placing a cap on the nipple, keeping the hammer at half-cock, he lifted the rifle to his shoulder and focused in on the warriors. As he had guessed, he was now certain these were Kiowa. Most of the warriors had the roached hairpiece that held feathers, the one thing that differentiated the Kiowa from others.

He watched as they came nearer, but when one of the leaders turned slightly and started barking orders to the others, he watched as they began to spread out and he knew they were definitely coming after them. He chose his first target, the warrior that rode to the right of the obvious leader, preferring to give the leader a chance to change his mind and lead his men away after he lost his closest warrior. He eared back the hammer to full cock, took a breath and let a little out, narrowed his sight and squeezed off his first shot.

The big blast of the .52 caliber Sharps split the quiet of the prairie, scattered the loose grass before him, and sent a lance of smoke from the muzzle. The big slug shattered the hairpipe breast plate of the warrior, causing him to jerk on the rein and bringing the horse high on his hind feet, unseating the rider, and dropping him in a clump.

The shock of the attack surprised and scattered the other warriors, but there was no cover for them, and Reuben quickly reloaded and sent another warrior to the other side of eternity. Several had slapped legs to their mounts, charging toward the shooter, lying low on the necks of their mounts, yet screaming their war cries and waving their weapons. Reuben fired again, but with his shot taking the horse in the chest, the warrior went flying over his head and fell headfirst into a big patch of prickly pear cactus, causing his war cries to immediately become much more enthusiastic!

As they neared, Reuben crabbed back from the crest and started back to where Elly waited, his long legs digging in his heels as he lunged and leaped to get to the bottom and cross the dry creek bed. As he neared the bottom, he was startled when two warriors from either side came charging toward him and Elly in the gravelly bottomed creek bed. Elly fired her Henry, dropping one man from his mount, and Reuben dropped to one knee, bringing up the Sharps and narrowing his sight on the nearest warrior. He dropped the hammer, the Sharps bucked, and the warrior screamed as the big slug shattered his solar plexus, driving him off his charging mount.

Elly's Henry barked again as Reuben hurried to

reload the Sharps. He was lifting the lever to close the breech when he heard two screams, one a war cry, the other in pain. He looked up to see Elly falling back, the feathered fletching of an arrow protruding from her upper chest. Wide-eyed, she stared at the warrior who had vaulted from his mount and was charging toward her, tomahawk raised high. Reuben snatched his Remington from the holster at his hip and swung it around as he brought it to full cock and pulled the trigger. The pistol spat smoke and lead to send the messenger of death to penetrate the warrior's side at the upraised arm. The tomahawk fell from limp fingers as the man seemed to melt into the sand and gravel.

Elly fell to her knees behind the big rock, her fingers grasping the shaft of the arrow. She looked up to see the last warrior charging toward Reuben, but her man stepped back and let the Remington bark again. The warrior took the slug in his throat, stifling his scream, and Reuben ran to Elly's side.

"There's more!" she moaned, fear showing in her eyes as she looked past Reuben, as five mounted warriors came charging down the slope toward them. Horses digging their front hooves in the loose soil, riders screaming, one trying to fire his rifle one handed, but the slug went clipping through the big juniper well away. Reuben grabbed his Henry, jacked a round in the chamber and dropped behind the big rock. He fired, jacked another round, fired again, and again and again. Smoke hung before them and he searched for another target, saw the shadowy figure of one, maybe two, driving their horses up the creek bed, trying to escape.

He stood up on the rock, searching for another target, anger driving him, fear filling him, not for himself, but for Elly. He looked down at her, leaning back against the big rock. She was breathing. He lifted his eyes again to search for any more warriors, but seeing and hearing none, he breathed deep and dropped from the rock, to go to her side. He went to one knee beside her and wiped the sweat and tears from his face, tenderly reaching for her wound, and moving her bloody hand away. He caught his breath, jumped to his feet to run, and retrieve the parfleche with medical supplies and quickly returned to her side.

18 / WOUND

Elly had turned slightly to her right side, leaning against the big rock, as Reuben examined the wound and the protruding arrow. "It went all the way through, which is a good thing. At least I won't have to cut out the arrowhead," he grumbled, nervously fidgeting as he examined the wound. He carefully began cutting away the buckskin tunic to expose the wound. Blood freely flowed from both the entry and the exit and Reuben shook his head as he explained, "I'm gonna hafta cut the shaft off 'bout here," as he held his hand at the entry wound. "I've gotta get it outta there 'fore I bandage it."

"I know that, just hurry up and get it done 'fore I pass out!" moaned Elly, gritting her teeth to the pain.

"Brace yourself," he instructed as he reached for the shaft. He let a breath out, "Maybe you better try to hold it tight," he suggested, "so it don't move so much." He was talking while he worked, the big blade of the Bowie cutting into the shaft of the arrow. He moved it at an angle, whittling away a tiny bit at a time. It was difficult to maneuver the big-bladed knife in such close quarters, but he continued, holding his breath until he made the last cut and leaned back. "I'm gonna break it off now," he explained as he held the short stub and the long shaft. He looked at Elly, saw her give a slight nod and clench her jaw. In one swift motion, he broke off the feathered end of the arrow and tossed it aside.

He shook his head and said, "This is the hard part. I'm gonna have to jerk it through from the back." He reached for a handful of bandages, giving some to Elly, "Hold this on that side, it'll prob'ly bleed pretty good."

"Before you do that, remember to use that balm," nodding to the parfleche, "in the canister. It's what's called the Balm of Gilead, made from the aspen buds in the spring. I put some buffalo root and sage with it, and it works quite well, so don't be stingy with it."

"I won't. I'll get you bandaged, then we're gonna get to the fort as quick as we can. They had a garrison doctor there, but if not, I'm sure Bent's wife will know a thing or two."

He took a patch of the buckskin scraps in the parfleche, folded it, and handed it to Elly. "Put that between your teeth, this is gonna hurt!" he instructed. She looked at him out of the corner of her eyes and said, "Just get it done and be quick about it."

She put the buckskin in her mouth, nodded and closed her eyes as she held the bandage to the entry wound. Reuben put the flat of his left palm against her back, the arrow protruding between his thumb and forefinger, wrapped a scrap of buckskin around the arrowhead and grasped it tightly. "Here goes!" and jerked the shaft through her back. Blood flowed freely from the wound, and he let it flow for a moment before reaching for the bandages and balm. With a liberal amount on both bandages, he started to apply it but Elly had slumped forward, her chin on her chest, unconscious.

He quickly applied the bandages, used the long strips of buckskin to wrap around her shoulder and chest to hold them tightly and satisfied, he gently leaned her back against the rock. He motioned for Bear to come close, and the big dog moved to her side, laying his head on her lap, and kept her upright and against the stone. Reuben quickly went to the horses, put the rifles in the scabbards, tightened the girths, and tied Daisy's reins to the tail of Blue, flipped the lead for the pack mule over his neck, and led the animals closer to Elly. He lifted Elly into the seat of his saddle, held her in place as he swung up behind her, and motioned for Bear to take the lead as they moved out. Reuben holding Elly before him, the mule came free rein like he often was wont to do, and Daisy kept pace, letting her rein fall slack between her and Blue's tail.

———

DUSK HAD DROPPED THE CURTAIN OF DARKNESS AS REUBEN nudged Blue into the water of the Arkansas River to cross over to Bent's ranch. He had been told there was no regimental surgeon at the fort and was encouraged to go to Bent's where Elly could at least get some care from Bent's woman, Island, the last of the three sisters that Bent had taken as his wives.

As they approached the stockade, Reuben hollered out, "Ho! I'm Reuben Grundy, a friend of William Bent! Is Mr. Bent home?"

"That's me, Reuben. The gate's open, c'mon in!" answered the familiar voice of Bent. Reuben pointed Blue to the gate and nudged him forward.

As they entered the compound, Bent stood aside and welcomed them. "She hurt?" he asked.

"Took a Kiowa arrow! I removed the arrow and bandaged her up some. She's been in and out ever since. Lost a lot of blood and needs some rest and maybe a woman's touch." He spoke as he swung down and lifted her from the horse.

"Take her on in the house, the spare room's on the left. I'll go get my woman and she can help take care of her," explained Bent, as he turned away and started to the hide lodges outside the stockade to fetch Island.

Reuben carried a weary Elly into the house, kicked open the door to the spare room and lay her on the bed. It was evident the bed had not been in use, and he pulled the covers from under her, laying them aside, as he began to strip the clothes from Elly. She moaned and struggled to move, the pain in her upper chest evident, but the bandages had stayed in place and he did his best to make her comfortable. As he lifted her head on the pillow, he spoke softly, "We're at Bent's house. His woman will be here soon and maybe she can help you."

Her eyes fluttered open, and she tried to smile, but winced at the pain and furrowed her brow. "Don't leave me."

"I won't. I'll be close by," he explained, turning to see Island come into the room.

Without speaking, Island nudged him aside and motioned for him to leave. She sat on the edge of the bed and began removing the bandage to examine the wound. As she lifted the compress, she frowned, touched the wound lightly and motioned for Reuben to bring the lamp closer.

He lifted the lamp, held it above the bed and watched as Island looked more closely at the wound. She touched it lightly, saw the beginning of a scab and glanced up at Reuben, nodding her approval. Island motioned for him to move the lantern aside so she could roll Elly to her side and examine the back wound. Satisfied, she rose and went to retrieve her bag of healing supplies.

It was just a short while and Island had finished cleaning the wound and applying fresh bandages. She spoke to Elly softly and rose to leave. "I will return with some soup for her. She must eat to keep up her strength and to heal."

Reuben nodded and stepped aside for the woman to leave. As Island disappeared through the doorway, Reuben sat beside Elly and reached up to touch her face. She looked at her man, gave a hint of a smile, and said, "I'll be alright. She is a good woman and will help me. You go on and put up the horses and do whatever you must."

Reuben nodded, "I'll be back shortly."

Bent waited in the front room and rose when Reuben came from the bedroom. "She goin' to be alright?"

"I think so. It'll be a while but she's a strong woman."

"Well, you stay here just as long as you need to, no need to leave anytime soon," answered Bent, motioning Reuben to a nearby chair.

"I've got to tend to the horses," started Reuben, motioning to the door.

"No need. I had one of the men take care of 'em. They'll bring your gear in here soon. Have a seat."

Reuben did as he was bidden and looked at Bent as he sat, "How'd it go with Black Kettle?"

"Good, good. The chiefs agreed, well all but Tall Bull and the Dog Soldiers, but they agreed to try for peace, and they'll have a man coming to the fort, prob'ly tomorrow, with a letter to Wynkoop for a council."

Reuben nodded, "We met Little Raven and he told us about the letter. He said they were willing to trade prisoners?"

"That's what they agreed. Now it's up to Wynkoop and the boys in blue," replied Bent.

"You think the Major will accept the terms?"

"Dunno, but I stopped at the fort earlier today and spoke with him to tell him what was coming, so, only time will tell. I hope they do!"

Reuben nodded his agreement, and asked, "Anything we can do?"

"I think the Major will at least listen, but he doesn't have much authority, none in fact, to try for a treaty. But I think he'll try to negotiate for one. Only time will tell." Bent rose, looked at Reuben, "Feel free to stay in here with your woman if you want, but I'm turning in for the night. It's been a long hard day of riding and I'm thinkin' tomorrow's gonna start mighty early!"

"Thanks Bill, I appreciate your help," answered Reuben, shaking the man's hand and turning back to Elly's room. He was determined to stay by her side as much as possible. They needed to be with one another at a time like this.

19 / LETTER

It was a restless night for Reuben, and he quietly picked his way from the room with Elly. Pushing open the front door, he walked out on the porch and breathed deep of the night air. After the stifling room and the smells of the wound dressing, he needed the freshness of the cool evening. Lifting his eyes to the sky, he let them wander over the many constellations he learned as a youth, his favorite being Orion. He and Elly had often looked heavenward and talked of the stars and Heaven beyond, and they chose the star at the tip of Orion's sword as *their* star. He smiled as he looked at the flickering light of the night, remembering the many times they lay together, holding hands, and praying. He moved to the steps, seating himself on the top step and with another lingering look to the lanterns of the stars, he began to pray. Each whispered word taken on the night breeze and lifted to the darkness dimpled by the flickering lights.

As he finished his prayer, he dropped his eyes to see a young man, sitting on his haunches in the middle of the compound, arms folded across his knees, and watching Reuben. The young man rose and came near, "You talk to your God in the darkness?"

Reuben nodded, motioning for the youth to be seated beside him, "Yes, I talk to my God at all times, night, day, anytime."

"And you believe He listens to you? He hears you?"

"Yes, I believe He always hears me."

"Does He talk to you?"

Reuben smiled, "Have you heard of the Bible?"

The young man frowned, shaking his head, and waited for more.

"The Bible is a book with many pages. On those pages are the words God has spoken to us, and when we read it, I believe the Spirit of God moves us to the right passages to answer what we seek. But even if it is not the answer we seek, His words guide us in our life."

"And you can hear these words?"

"We can *read* these words. Have you ever seen the words of the white man on paper?"

"I have seen *Little White Man* with what you say."

"*Little White Man?*"

"The one you call Bent, he who has this big lodge," motioning to the house behind them.

Reuben grinned, nodding, "I am called Man with the Blue Horse. I was given that name by Little Raven, chief of the Arapaho."

"I am Blue Turtle. I live with Island. My mother and father died of the white man's spotted disease and my grandfather, White Thunder, told Island and Yellow Woman to take me, but Yellow Woman left to join the Dog Soldiers."

Reuben looked at the young man, guessing him to be

about twelve summers. It was a cool night and everyone else was asleep, yet this young man was wandering about, wearing only moccasins and a breech cloth. "My wife, Yellow Bird, is inside. Island has bandaged her wound and made some broth for her. We are friends of Bent and will be here for a while. Perhaps we can talk again of this Bible, and I can show you how God tells us about Heaven and what we must do to make it to Heaven. Would you want to know about that?"

"Yes. Island is a good healer. She will make your woman better and we can talk about this white man's book of many words." He stood, looking down at the still seated Reuben, "I will return," and walked away across the compound and through the big gates.

———

IT WAS EARLY MORNING WHEN REUBEN AND BENT SAT ON the porch, watching the long shadows begin to retrace their steps as the sun slowly rose off their right shoulder. Bent looked at Reuben, "Wynkoop will prob'ly have some scouts out lookin' for the ones comin' with the letter I tol' him about. I just hope they're peaceable with 'em. I know both One Eye and Eagle Head, they're pretty easy goin' but some o' them wet behind the ears sojer boys can get a man's dander up mighty easy!"

"It don't make no difference what color of skin they have or uniform they're wearin', there's always some that have short fuses and seem to blow up at just about anything!"

"Maybe we should go down and see if they need an interpreter or somethin'," suggested Bent, looking askance at Reuben.

Reuben glanced toward Bent, nodded, and stood. "I'll

see 'bout Elly, maybe you could have the boy bring our horses 'round?'

"I'll just do that," responded Bent, standing to go fetch the boy and the horses.

———

IF IT WERE ON A PALATIAL HOME IN THE SOUTH, IT WOULD be a veranda. But here in the middle of Fort Lyon, the commandant's quarters shared a covered porch with the office of Major Wynkoop. It was on the porch, enjoying the shade from the warm morning sun, where Wynkoop, Captain Soule, Bent and Reuben Grundy sat discussing the offer made by the Southern Cheyenne chiefs led by Black Kettle, and the Arapaho chiefs, led by Little Raven.

"When I first read the letter, it sounded like a demand for ransom for the captives, but when One Eye and Eagle Head said that Black Kettle and Left Hand traded personal goods for the prisoners, I had to take another look at the wording of the letter." He paused, looked at Bent, "Weren't you there when they put that together?"

"Yeah, but they had my son, George, translate and write it. I never read it, but he told me what it said, and I think the chiefs were all sincere in their wanting peace," replied William Bent, leaning forward, elbows on his knees as he looked at the two men. "But I think they were wanting the letter to go to you and Agent Colley."

"Sam Colley had a little too much to drink and won't be joinin' us till later. How much later I don't know," added the Major, shaking his head in disgust at the continued antics of the less than honorable Indian agent. It had long been rumored that Colley cheated the Indians of their many rations, handing them off to his son, Dexter, who was a trader who made immense profits when selling the goods that rightfully belonged to the Indians. The major looked up at Bent, glanced to Reuben, and asked, "What do you think of this proposal?"

Bent leaned back, a stoic expression painting his face, "Like I said, I think they mean what they propose, but you need to remember, that letter does not include the Sioux, Comanche, and Kiowa. And the bulk of the Dog Soldiers chose to follow Tall Bull and left the council."

"So, you think there's a chance for peace with those that come to the council?"

"I do. It is a first step, and this is under the leadership of Black Kettle, a very respected chief of the Cheyenne. The other treaties have usually been initiated by the soldiers and politicians or land grabbers, and as you know, they've been broken every time. But the chiefs are weary of war, their women wail at the loss of their young warriors, and many lodges are without a man and the women and children are hungry." Bent shook his head as he pictured the villages with empty lodges, looked up at the Major, "I think this is a good opportunity for the beginning of peace."

"I know much of the raiding and killing that has happened in the last couple months has been by the Dog Soldiers, am I right?"

"You are," replied Bent. "But there have been others as you know, especially down here in the southern part of the territory. It's been mostly the Kiowa and Comanche."

Reuben scooted forward on his chair, leaning into the conversation, "Little Raven led the Arapaho and the Cheyenne to make peace with the Kiowa and Comanche. I think if this," nodding to the letter in Wynkoop's hand, "works like we hope, Little Raven can be influential in bringing the Kiowa and Comanche to the table to talk peace as well."

As quiet seemed to take the men's thoughts inward, Captain Soule spoke up, "This was the first time I've been in talks with the leaders, and I must admit, I was impressed with the men. When One Eye told you," looking to Wynkoop, "that even though he feared being killed by coming to the fort, he was willing to die to make peace. That kinda changed my thinking about these people. I used to think they were ignorant heathen and only worthy of being wiped off the land, I'm beginning to realize I was wrong."

Wynkoop looked from Bent to Reuben and back, "One Eye said Black Kettle's Cheyenne bands have to keep on the move to avoid Chivington's attacks, is that right?"

"Ummhmmm, all the bands are staying on the move," answered Reuben.

"So, it's best if we get this done right away, to free the captives before something bad happens," resolved Wynkoop. He looked at his subordinate, Captain Soule, "Let's see if we can muster enough volunteers to go with us to the Smoky Hill and get the captives. Maybe we can talk the chiefs into taking another step toward peace." He looked at Bent, "Will you go with us?"

"I will. And because of Reuben's friendship with Little Raven, it might be good if he comes along as well," suggested Bent.

Wynkoop looked at Reuben, nodded, "We'll be pullin' out first thing in the mornin'!"

"We'll be ready!" declared Reuben, glancing to Bent who nodded his agreement.

———

As the two men went to their horses, Reuben asked Bent, "Alright if Elly stays at your home?"

"Of course. Island has kinda taken to her and I think they'd like the time to get to know each other," answered Bent. "And they'll be safe there, so you won't need to worry about her."

20 / RESPONSE

Reuben looked to his left and asked One Eye, "You are Cheyenne and Eagle Head is of the Bowstrings of the Cheyenne, were there no Arapaho at your council?" The two men rode side by side, following Eagle Head who was sided by Bent. With Major Wynkoop and Captain Soule in the lead, the long column to two-by stretched behind them. The major told the others there were one hundred thirty volunteers of the Colorado First Cavalry from Fort Lyon who wanted to be a part of what some thought would be a history making event, but there were some who could be heard grumbling about the 'dirty redskins' that needed to be wiped from the earth. Some agreed with Chivington who often said the only way to deal with Indians is to *kill them!* The same men also echoed the words of Governor Evans *"To go in pursuit of all hostile Indians... to kill and destroy as enemies of this country, wherever they may be found."*

Reuben had heard the grumblings when he and Bent came from the house into the compound of the fort and the men were readying their mounts. Few paid any attention to them as they rode in and continued their grumblings as they passed. Reuben had asked Bent, "Didn't the Major say they were getting volunteers?"

"He did, but you know how *volunteers* are encouraged in the army. There's very little real volunteering to it!" chuckled Bent as they passed the grumblers.

Now the column of volunteers was enroute to the agreed upon meeting site on the Smoky Hill River and Reuben was trying to find out more from the messenger, One Eye.

"Yes, there were some. Little Raven and Left Hand were the chiefs from the Arapahos, but Black Kettle, White Antelope and War Bonnet of the Cheyenne were the leaders of the council," explained One Eye. The Cheyenne warrior carried himself aloof and proud, though the scar across his forehead and cheek was the constant reminder of the battle that had robbed him of his eye and changed his name. It had been a raid on the Pawnee and his band of raiders had taken the horse herd of more than a hundred horses, but the battle that occurred when the Pawnee caught up with them, had been a costly but victorious fight. One Eye had fought bravely, killing five of the Pawnee, and his reputation as a warrior was forever grounded in the history of his people.

"Little Raven and his people are close friends. It was Little Raven that gave the ceremony when my woman, Yellow Bird, and I were joined. His women became close with my woman. They are good people."

"Little Raven has always been known as a leader that seeks peace, but his son has joined with the Dogmen of the Cheyenne and makes war against the intruders into our land."

"I have met the young Little Raven. He fights well."

One Eye twisted around to look at Reuben, wondering about the white man who spoke of the fighting ability of Little Raven. Such words are usually only spoken by those that have fought against the one of whom they speak.

Reuben saw the questioning look on One Eye's face and let a slight grin show as he shook his head, "No, I did not fight him personally, but we met up and shared some meat with him and his men."

One Eye nodded, glanced to those that led the column and told Reuben, "I must speak with Wynkoop before we go further." Without another word, he clamped his legs to his mount and trotted the animal to the side of Wynkoop. As he neared the Major he began, "My people have been attacked by soldiers before and do not know you. We are near the Smoky Hill River and there will be many times more of our warriors than you have soldiers. Maybe as many as 2000 warriors. If they believe you come to fight, you will die. It is best if we tell Black Kettle that you come in peace."

"Then go!" directed Wynkoop, motioning with his hand toward the distant river. One Eye turned to Eagle Head and motioned him to go. As the man slapped legs to his mount to kick him into a canter, Wynkoop looked sidelong at Captain Soule, "Did you hear what he said?"

"Yessir. I don't cotton to mixin' it up with no 2000 warriors!"

One Eye had dropped back to ride beside Reuben and explained what he had told the Major. Reuben frowned and asked, "Black Kettle has that many warriors?"

"There are the warriors of War Bonnet and White Antelope and of my village. There are also those of Little Raven and Left Hand and the Dogmen of Bull Bear and Eagle Head. I do not know if there are Sioux or others."

As they neared the river, Black Kettle had aligned his warriors two deep along the north shore of the river, the defensive line stretching more than a hundred yards to either side and presented a formidable sight. Wynkoop immediately passed the order to Soule who relayed it to the First Sergeant, who barked, "By a column of fours! Rifles at the ready!" The long column quickly moved into the new broader formation, each man slipping his Spencer from the scabbard by his knee and sitting the rifle butt on his thigh, holding the weapon steady but in sight.

The First Sergeant barked, "Columns one and two, form two ranks to the left, HO!" and quickly followed with "Columns three and four, form two ranks to the right, HO!" At the commands the men swung to the side, forming two skirmish lines, but remained on their horses, immobile, awaiting another command. "Trooooop halt!" bringing the two ranks to a halt, horses trying to prance but held in check by the cavalrymen. The ranks of soldiers eyed the many warriors on the far bank, each warrior sitting with a stoic expression and staring at the resented soldiers. The men in blue knew they were badly outnumbered and each one had similar thoughts that they did not want to get in a fight today. Although less than the projected 2000, there were easily 800 warriors, ready and willing to engage the soldiers.

Little did Wynkoop know that these were all Black Kettle's warriors, but word had been sent to the camps of the Arapaho and the Sioux. The Major motioned to One Eye and brought him close, "You go talk to Black Kettle, see what he wants to do about this council. We'll wait here."

One Eye nodded and kicked his mount into a canter. He splashed across the shallow creek and rode directly to Black Kettle. With a glance to Bull Bear, the Dog Soldier leader, One Eye nodded and said, "Major Wynkoop desires a council to talk peace. What do you want?'

Black Kettle looked at his friend, One Eye, "Eagle Head has told of the coming of Wynkoop. Tell him to take his soldiers back to Wild Horse Creek, camp there. We will go back to our camps beyond the river. We will come to him soon. You return after you tell him."

One Eye nodded, reined his mount around and kicked it to a canter, splashed across the river and quickly came beside the Major and delivered the message. Wynkoop looked from One Eye to the chiefs across the river, nodded, and passed the order to Captain Soule. The Sergeant barked out, "By a column of twos! Rifles in the scabbards – To the rear – HO!" The two ranks melted into the two columns and started away from the river. The Major, Captain, Bent and Reuben kicked their mounts to a canter and quickly passed the column to take the lead again. As they dropped to a walk, Wynkoop twisted around in his saddle to look behind them, nodded and said, "They're leavin'!"

Captain Soule was the first to respond, "That makes it a little easier to breathe!"

The others chuckled, agreeing, although nothing needed to be said.

―――――

IT WAS A SMALL CREEK, BUT THE WATER WAS CLEAR AND cool and ample for the horses and men. They made a comfortable camp with the only shelter the cottonwoods and willows that lined the small creek. Most gathered about the clusters of sage and the few random piñon or juniper. As dusk dropped its curtain, small cookfires twinkled to life to dot the desolate flats, offering a semblance of comfort to the camping soldiers. Reuben and Bent made their camp slightly apart from the soldiers, and with the small coffee pot dancing beside the fire, the glow of the firelight painted their faces as they sat back, pondering what had already happened, and what they hoped might happen in the coming days. Reuben looked at Bent, "Hopeful, are you?"

"Ummhmm, I'm hopeful. And I'm tired. I've spent most of my life on this prairie in the company of many of the same people that have been making war, and I'm tired. After this gets settled, I think I'll go back east. I've got a little farm and it'd make a nice place to sit on the porch and enjoy the sunsets without fear of getting my hair lifted!"

"Sounds reasonable," answered Reuben. He stared at the flames, something he had always tried to avoid, but thoughts chased each other through his mind, and he looked up at Bent. "Me'n the missus have decided we're gonna turn in these badges and skedaddle outta here. Evans and his kind can have their politics and such. We're done with it!"

21 / COUNCIL

The eastern sky blushed pink as the slow rising sun betrayed a cloudless sky and the buffalo grass was tinged with color as the morning breeze whispered across the flatlands. In the distance, a few scant miles away, the shadowy figures of many riders slowly approached the makeshift camp of the Fort Lyon soldiers. One of the two guards that stood in the shadows of the gnarly cottonwoods shouted, "Riders comin'!"

Major Wynkoop and Captain Soule moved to the edge of the camp that face to the northeast, shading their eyes as they looked across the flats to see the riders coming. "Must be the chiefs, comin' as they promised," declared Wynkoop, turning back to the camp. Several men had been put to work fashioning a brush arbor and he spoke to them, "Get some blankets, cover the ground there." He turned to others that sat near their scant cookfires anticipating a bit of coffee for the morning, "You men," motioning to a group of five soldiers, "take your places at the edge of the willows and hold your fire, they're comin' for peace talks." He turned to face the rest of the camp, "Now men, stay on your guard, keep your weapons near, but don't even look like you're wantin' to fight. There's not as many of them this time, but you saw how many warriors they have and if they were to decide to, they could overtake us and we wouldn't stand a chance. So, keep your tempers in check and obey orders! Do I make myself clear!"

The men stirred about, answering with 'yessir' as they moved into their places, but grumbling was always the way of soldiers, and the undercurrent of dissent was obvious. The men had been assigned places the night before and with the top sergeant directing them, they were soon in their defensive positions as directed. The Major walked to where Bent and Reuben had made their camp and with a lowered voice, he asked, "Could you men stay close, listen and make sure the translation we get is accurate?"

Bent nodded, "We will, but I see they have my son, George, with them, and he'll give you an honest translation."

"I'm sure *he* will, but I also recognized John Smith and he's about as crooked as a dog's hind leg! Him and Colley have been in cahoots for some time and been cheatin' the Indians out of their annuities, takin' the goods and tradin' or sellin' 'em. But I've been so busy with the raids and such, I haven't been able to catch 'em at it. So, I just don't trust the man."

Bent nodded, glanced to Reuben, "I'll be near the Cheyenne, Reuben here will be close to the Arapaho, so we'll do what we can, Major."

The Major frowned, looking at Bent, "Any advice?"

"Just be honest and firm. Black Kettle's a tough man, but a great leader and a fair man. He's the one you need to pay attention to, he'll influence the others."

Wynkoop nodded, turned on his heel and crossed the camp to welcome the visitors.

———

AS THE CHIEFS FILED INTO THE CAMP, THEIR WARRIORS took their horses and stayed near the tree line, keeping their distance but close enough to be brought into action at the wave of a hand. Black Kettle led the small entourage, following Major Wynkoop who motioned them to the blankets under the brush arbor. Black Kettle seated himself, motioning the others to take their places. To the right of Black Kettle sat Bull Bear, the leader of the Dogmen. On his left, White Antelope, and One Eye, both chiefs of their villages, seated themselves. To the right of Bull Bear, Little Raven and Left Hand sat, representing the Arapaho peoples.

Wynkoop sat directly opposite Black Kettle, Captain Soule on his right before White Antelope and One Eye. To the left of the Major sat Lieutenants Cramer and Phillips. George Bent and John Smith stood behind the chiefs, and William Bent and Reuben, stood behind the soldiers.

Wynkoop began, holding the letter proposing peace before him, "I know this letter says you want peace and tells of captives you want to trade, yet you meet us with a great number of warriors as if you prepare for war. I want to know what prisoners you have and about the attacks by your people that captured these people."

The chiefs looked at one another, stern scowls showing as they spoke among themselves, but Black Kettle quickly quieted them with an uplifted hand. "What fights do you ask about?"

Wynkoop nodded, dropped his eyes, looked up at the

chief and began, "We found two men murdered and scalped downriver from Fort Lyon, some believe it was young Little Raven and his men. Before that, there was the attack on the big wagon train near Cimarron Crossing, where ten," holding up both hands with all fingers extended, "men were killed, their bodies mutilated, and many more were wounded, the wagon master killed and wagons burnt."

Chief Black Kettle raised his hand to stop Wynkoop, and nodded, "The fighting you speak of was Kiowa." The other chiefs nodded, and mumbled words of agreement, "But you speak of these fights while your soldier chief Curtis, from Fort Kearney, and his many soldiers, as many as all my warriors, search the land to the rising sun for my people, wanting to fight and kill all that he finds!"

"I know nothing of what General Curtis does, and I have no authority over him. But I cannot talk peace with my commanders when all they know is the killing and taking of captives by your warriors!" declared Wynkoop, visibly upset as he squirmed in his seat, forcing himself to stay seated. "And it was not Kiowa that attacked Jimmy's Camp on the Platte, killing those that fought. And it was your son," looking directly at Little Raven of the Arapaho, "that attacked the wagon below Fort Lyon, killed the man and stole his mules and captured his wife!"

Chief Black Kettle snarled, slowly shaking his head, "All that you say has happened, but your soldier chief, Chivington, has attacked villages and killed our people. And we sent a letter before this," motioning to the letter in Wynkoop's hand, "to your Fort, but you sent soldiers against my people when you chased Neva and his warriors away! It was only the storm from the Creator that stopped your soldiers from killing my warriors!"

Voices had been raised, anger was boiling, and all were getting restless, until William Bent and Reuben stepped from behind the soldiers and stood between the leaders. Bent had his hands raised and said, "Whoa, hold on!" looking from the Indians to the soldiers. "Didn't you come together to talk peace? Not to rehash the things of the past?" He stood before Wynkoop, his back to the chiefs, "These chiefs have come to offer captives as a token of peace, you won't get them by arguing!"

Wynkoop took a deep breath, his shoulders slumped, and he motioned Bent aside. As Bent stepped away, Reuben did also, and the Major said, "He's right. I just can't see talking peace when there are captives involved. Here's what I propose, if you will deliver the captives promptly, we can talk further of peace. Now, you must know, I do not have the authority to secure a treaty, but if the captives are delivered, I promise I will escort you and the chiefs to our big chief, Governor Evans, in Denver City, for a peace council with him."

Black Kettle looked from one chief to another until he had received a nod of agreement from each one. He faced Wynkoop, "You stay at this camp. We will deliver the captives within two days. It will take time to get them and to talk to the other chiefs about this talk with your big chief."

Wynkoop nodded, extending his hand to shake with Black Kettle who accepted the offer and the two men stood, shook hands, and the chiefs walked from the camp. As they mounted their horses, none looked back to the soldiers, as that was not the way of the people, and the entire party rode back to the northeast, a wispy dust cloud trailing behind.

———

BENT AND THE OTHERS WALKED TO THE NEARBY CAMPFIRE and accepted offered cups of coffee from the Corporal in charge of the cooking. As they stood around the small cookfire, Bent looked to Wynkoop, "I think you've done well, Major. Black Kettle is determined to have peace and will return with the captives soon. But did you plan this trip to the Governor before this?"

Wynkoop chuckled, "I did not. And the only ones that have the authority to make a treaty are General Curtis or General Blunt. But of course, Evans is the Superintendent of Indian Affairs and I guess he has the authority."

"Uh, do either of the generals know about this?" asked Reuben,

"Nope! But if I had tried to get them involved, it would take many days, if not weeks, and by that time, I don't think the chiefs would be in agreement."

"So, you're going to just march into Denver uninvited?" asked Bent.

Wynkoop chuckled, nodding his head, "I guess that about sums it up!"

22 / CHANGES

Reuben looked from Bent to the Major, "Well, I don't see where I'm needed here, so if it's alright with you gentlemen, I think I'll head out and go see my woman, make sure she's healin' up like we hope."

Wynkoop looked at Reuben, "I did not know your wife was ill."

"Not ill, she's healin' up from a Kiowa arrow," explained Reuben.

The Major frowned, "When did this happen?"

"A few days back, let's see, it was three days 'fore we left the fort to come on this little jaunt. We had been to see Little Raven and a band of Kiowa jumped us. I think they were returning from a raid or a hunt or somethin'. They were headin' south when they crossed our tracks and were drivin' some stolen horses. Reckon they thought they could add ours to their bunch, but it didn't quite work out that way for 'em."

"How many?" asked Captain Soule.

"How many what? How many there were, or how many were left?"

The Major chuckled, "I think he was wonderin' how many attacked *and* how many were left."

"'Bout a dozen, give or take, but only about four or five were left," stated Reuben without explaining or bragging. It was never a matter of pride when he spoke about taking the life of another man, regardless of color.

"You killed eight?" asked Soule, doubt written on his face.

"No, me and my woman killed eight, maybe nine. But one of 'em got too close, put an arrow in her and thought he'd take her hair, but I convinced him otherwise." He paused, lifted his eyes to the Major, "So, if you've no objection, I think I'll skedaddle."

The Major nodded, "Thanks for your help, Reuben."

"My pleasure, Major. Here's hopin' all this turns into peace!" added Reuben as he turned away and started for their camp.

———

HE RODE THE SUN DOWN AND STOPPED FOR A SHORT REST and a bite to eat but was soon on the trail again. He enjoyed the night with its muted sounds and stillness. The big moon was waxing full, and his eyes soon adjusted to the dim light. Blue seemed to lengthen his stride as they moved across the moonlit flatlands, the buffalo grass swaying in the night breeze. The shadowy clumps of sage and greasewood mimicked the hump-backed buffalo, the long-eared jackrabbits bounded away at their passing, and the distant cry of a lonesome coyote was carried by the gliding wings of the night birds. He stopped at the banks of a small gurgling creek and let Blue take his drink as he listened to the arguing bullfrogs that inhabited the marsh at the big bend of the creek.

It was a peaceful night, but as he stood beside Blue, his hand resting on the big roan's mane, Reuben's hackles marched up his neck and he caught his breath. There was danger near, the night birds were silent, and the bullfrogs were stilled. Blue lifted his head, his ears pricked and nostrils flaring as he turned his head to look behind him. Reuben unbuttoned his jacket and dropped his hand to the butt of his Remington pistol as he casually turned his back to the roan to search the surrounding flats by the dim light of the moon.

The screamed war cry split the night as the shadow sprang from the willows, leaping high, arms outstretched and feet pedaling the air as the crazed warrior, one hand holding a war club, the other a knife whose metal blade appeared to shimmer in the moonlight. The warrior crashed into Reuben, driving him against Blue, but the horse held his stance and gave Reuben his strength to stand. Reuben dragged the pistol from the holster as he turned to face the onslaught, but the figure was upon him before he could bring it to bear. He lifted it high to block the knife wielding hand and ducked under the war club. The club struck the seat of the saddle as Reuben brought up his knee, driving it into the attacker's groin. Reuben pushed the man back with his left hand and forced down the warriors left hand that held the knife.

The warrior's face was contorted, eyes blazing, his mouth and nose in a snarl as he screamed his war cry. He raised his war club high for another blow, but Reuben drove the muzzle of his pistol against the man's ribs and dropped the hammer. The Remington roared its muffled blast, burning the man's skin with its blazing powder and driving the slug into the man's side. The warrior staggered back, dropping his knife, and putting his hand to the wound. His eyes flared again, and he raised the war club, but Reuben cocked the Remington and fired again, the bullet shattering the hair pipe bone breast plate and driving into the man's chest. The warrior stumbled, his war club slipping from his hand, and with hate-filled eyes, he snarled at Reuben and dropped to his knees to fall forward on his face.

Reuben fell back against Blue, gasping for air, and lowered his pistol. He carefully lowered the hammer and returned the pistol to the holster. He shook his head, mumbled to Blue, "You coulda warned me a little sooner, Blue."

He stepped closer to the body and with his foot, rolled the man to his back. He recognized the man as a Kiowa, his roach hair, braids, and markings on his arms, told of his tribe. Sightless eyes stared at the stars, his mouth still in a snarl, but a jagged wound that traveled from the man's ear, down his neck, to his chest, marked the man as a warrior that had been wounded and perhaps left behind by his fellow warriors, believing him to be dead. The long and deep cut had festered, dried blood showed black in the moonlight, and another blackened wound showed on the man's leg that was bent under him. *This man's been in a fight, prob'ly earlier today.*

Reuben lifted his eyes to the east, saw the faint grey line of early morning, and his first thoughts were of Elly. He did not expect the renegades to attack Bent's home, but he also knew in these times, anything could happen. He grabbed the reins, slipped one over Blue's neck and swung back into the saddle. "Let's go boy, we need to check on Elly!"

It was mid-morning when he came within sight of the Fort, and nothing appeared to be amiss. The gate stood open, the horse herd was grazing contentedly in the pasture, and soldiers were seen atop the ramparts. Reuben took the trail that bypassed the fort and went to the crossing of the Arkansas River. Although the water was swift moving, it was not very deep, touching the bottoms of Reuben's stirrups at its deepest. As Blue came from the water, Reuben stepped down and let the big roan shake off the excess water but knew the horse would not attempt to roll with the saddle. The big horse stood, bent his head around to look at Reuben and watched as he mounted.

Within moments, they rode into the compound of the small stockade of Bent's home. Elly was sitting in a rocker, a blanket across her lap, and with a broad smile, waved at Reuben as he came into the compound. She did not stand, which told Reuben of her condition, and he quickly reined up, dropped the reins to ground tie Blue, and bounded up the steps to greet his woman. He dropped to his knee beside the chair, reached out to cradle her chin in his hands, kissed her hello and said, "How you doin'?"

"Fine now!" she answered, giggling at her concerned man. "How are you?"

"Fine now!" he answered, chuckling. He stood, pulled a ladder-back chair beside her and sat down, taking her hand in his. "How's the wound?"

"Healing nicely. Island has been wonderful and she's very skilled with things. I've been in good hands. Now, tell me about the peace council, how'd it go?"

Reuben grinned, dropping his eyes, then looked up at her and began to narrate the happenings of the last few days. As he finished his tale, he leaned back, "So, the chiefs should be coming to the fort soon, and the Major will be taking them to the Governor to try to make a treaty for peace."

"Did they bring in the captives?" asked Elly.

"Dunno. They were supposed to, but I left before that... kinda anxious to get back and see how you were doin'!" he declared, smiling as he leaned forward to give her another kiss.

As they talked, Island came up on the porch, arms full of bandages and ointments. When she saw Reuben, she asked, "Did Bent come with you?"

"No, he'll be back in a day or two. He stayed to help with the translation."

She nodded, knowingly, and sat the bundle down to come to the side of her patient. She waved Reuben away and he stood, nodding, and smiling to his wife, and went down the steps to tend to his horse. In the barn, Reuben stripped the gear from Blue and rubbed him down with a handful of hay, scooped him some grain into the bin and put him in a stall. As he began putting the gear away in the tack room, the young Cheyenne boy, Blue Turtle, came into the barn and watched as Reuben stowed the gear.

"You have been with the chiefs?" he asked, his stoic face revealing nothing.

"Yes. Bent and I went with the soldiers to talk to the chiefs from the Southern Cheyenne and the Arapaho, to discuss a peace treaty."

"What chiefs did you meet?"

"Black Kettle, White Antelope, One Eye and Bull Bear."

"Black Kettle is a great leader," stated Blue Turtle.

"Yes, he is, and he led the council. I believe it will be a good treaty," surmised Reuben as he came from the tack room. "But, what about you, have you thought about what we talked about? The Bible book that tells about God?"

"Yes. I have thought about it, and I would like to know more."

Reuben nodded, returned to the gear, and retrieved his Bible from the saddle bags. He stepped beside Turtle and said, "Let's go to the porch and we'll talk."

They sat side by side on the long bench and Reuben opened his Bible and began to explain about writing, letters, and words. "As these letters are arranged, they form the words. And the words were given by God to show us how to live." He looked at Turtle and saw his look of amazement and continued, "Now, I want to show you the words that tell us about ourselves and our future and what God says about what he has prepared for us," and began flipping through the pages. He stopped at John 14:2 and said, "Now, this is where He tells us about what He has for us in Heaven." He began to read the last part of verse one, *Ye believe in God, believe also in me. In my Father's house are many mansions, if it were not so, I would have told you. I go to prepare a place for you.*

As Reuben paused, Turtle asked, "Mansions?"

Reuben smiled, nodding, "Yes, a mansion is a big fancy house, like this" pointing back to Bent's house, "but bigger and better. That's His way of giving us hope for the future. But," he paused and began turning the pages again, stopping at the book of Romans, "He also tells us what we must know about how to make sure of Heaven as our home."

Reuben paused as he saw Turtle frown and cock his head to the side, "Heaven?"

"Yes. That's the place God has in store for us, if we do as He says. Some native people call it 'the Other Side', some say that's where we go when we take the starry road, what we call the Milky Way, and go to the place of the Great Spirit, or Wakan Tanka, of Gitche Manitou."

His expression slowly changed as Blue Turtle began to understand and nodded his head. He looked at Reuben, pointed to the book on his lap and said, "Tell me more."

"First, He tells us in Romans 3:23 *For all have sinned and come short of the glory of God.* Sinned means the wrong that we do, you know, like hurting others, telling things that are not true, not doing what our mothers say, like that. Do you understand? Have you ever done those things that are wrong?"

Turtle dropped his eyes and slowly nodded his head, mumbling the words "Yes, I have done those things. I know it is wrong."

"Good, that's what He tells us, when we do wrong, we come short, or miss out on the glory of God, or Heaven. Now the next thing, He reminds us what happens when we do wrong, in chapter five and verse 12, *Wherefore as by one man, sin entered into the world, and death by sin, and so death passed upon all men, for that all have sinned.* He reminds us that we have sinned, or done those wrong things, but He also tells us because of that, there is a penalty or punishment for that, and that penalty is death."

"But, everyone dies, do they not?" asked Turtle.

"Yes, but that's not just dying and being buried, that is the eternal death, or what the Bible calls going to Hell for punishment forever. But the worst part is, that would mean we never make it to the place of the Great Spirit, and God does not want that, so..." he paused as he turned the pages.

"Here in chapter six and verse 23 He adds, *For the wages of sin is death; but the gift of God is eternal life through Jesus Christ our Lord.* See, He says because of the bad we've done, we deserve that death, or complete separation from the Great Spirit and Heaven, but He doesn't want that for us, so he offers us a gift—that gift is eternal life, it's a gift that was paid for by Jesus when He died on the cross to pay that penalty for us, so we would have the opportunity to live forever in Heaven with Him."

Turtle frowned, and asked, "Eternal life?"

"Yes. Eternal means forever, never to end. To have life forever is to live forever with the one who gives that gift. He also tells us how to get that gift. Now look here in chapter ten, verse nine, *That if thou shalt confess with thy mouth the Lord Jesus, and shalt believe in thine heart that God hath raised him from the dead, thou shalt be saved. For with the heart man believeth unto righteousness; and with the mouth, confession is made unto salvation. For whosoever shall call upon the name of the Lord, shall be saved.* It's just that simple, to believe with your heart these things that I've read—to know we're sinners, and because we're sinners we deserve death and hell forever, but God paid for the gift of eternal life so we could know Heaven as our home and all we have to do it to believe it and ask for the gift of eternal life. Do you understand that?"

Turtle frowned, his expression telling that he was thinking about what he had been told and he began to show his thoughts and understanding and slowly nodded his head. "I do. It is easy to know and to believe on God or the Great Creator, or Wakan Tanka. He has done this for us, and we can have that gift if we ask for it."

"Would you like to do that now? Ask for the gift, I mean?"

"Yes, I would."

"Then let's bow our heads, and I will pray and show you what to do, then you can pray and ask for that gift."

Turtle followed Reuben's example, listened while he prayed...

"Our Heavenly Father, we come to you now so Blue Turtle can receive..." and he continued to remind Turtle of the need to understand he was a sinner, there was a penalty for that sin, that Christ paid the penalty and in doing that, purchased the gift of eternal life for everyone that would truly believe with their heart and ask for and receive that gift. As Turtle listened, Reuben then asked, "Turtle, if you want to receive that gift, and you believe with your whole heart in what the Bible says, then repeat after me this simple prayer... Dear God, I want to trust you today to forgive me of my sins, and to come into my life and give me that gift of eternal life. I want to trust Jesus as my Savior and to have that gift of eternal life to go to Heaven with you when I die. Thank you God for that gift. In Jesus Name I pray, Amen."

As they finished the prayer, they looked at one another and let a slow smile paint their faces. Turtle looked at Reuben, "This is a good thing. Would you teach me how to know these letters and words so I too can know what God says?"

Reuben grinned, "I will do what I can while I'm here, but I will also find someone at the fort that can also teach you."

Turtle nodded, stood, and said, "I must tell Island, she is a mother to me and must know these things also."

Reuben nodded and watched as the young man left, anxious to tell others about his new knowledge and experience with the God of the Bible. He smiled as he thought about how simple it is and the truth of it that when someone comes to know Christ, they are anxious to share that simple truth.

23 / CONCERNS

The dust cloud rose high in the northern sky. With no breeze on the desert flats, buffalo grass stood tall, rabbit brush with the new yellow blossoms did not wave at the passersby, and the sage failed to nod their hoary heads to the many riders. Major Wynkoop and William Bent rode beside Black Kettle and Bull Bear, the chiefs of the Cheyenne and the Dog Soldiers. Behind the leaders rode a disheveled Laura Roper, the sixteen-year-old young woman that had been held captive by the Dog Soldiers and traded for by Left Hand, chief of the Arapaho. As she had before, Laura continued to look after the three children, Isabel Eubank, Ambrose Asher, and Dan Marble, who had also been captives of the Dog Soldiers and were traded for by Left Hand.

Bent looked to Major Wynkoop, "I think I'll leave you here, Major. I'm goin' to my home and check on my family and Reuben and his woman. If you need me, you know where I'll be and just send a messenger."

"Well, like we discussed Mr. Bent, we're just goin' to freshen up a bit, let these troopers change duties with some others, then we'll be headin' out to Denver City to meet with the governor. We'll probably rest up tonight and leave 'bout sunrise. If you change your mind and want to come along, you'll be welcome!" explained the Major.

"That's quite alright, Major. What with Neva, Bosse, and Knock Knee ridin' behind us all the way, my scalp was constantly itching, and I've had enough of that!" chuckled Bent, although he knew he was in no danger from any of the chiefs that traveled with them, but Bull Bear of the Dog Soldiers kept giving him a once-over stare that made him have second thoughts about his safety. With a wave over his shoulder, Bent reined away from the group and pointed his big bay horse to the river crossing and home.

While Wynkoop, Captain Soule, and the Lieutenants led the soldiers and chiefs into the compound of Fort Lyon, William Bent pushed his gelding into the water to cross the Arkansas. Once across the river and away from the bosque, he rode the big bay up the slight hill and into his stockade, stepped down and handed his horse off to Blue Turtle to put him away. Reuben stood on the porch, watching the return of Bent and grinned as he bounded up the steps to shake his hand. "Good to see you back, Bill," declared Reuben, stepping back to the chair he had vacated. Bent dropped into the chair beside him and breathed deep of the clear air, content to be home.

As Island brought the men fresh cups of coffee and handed them off, Reuben asked, "Did Little Raven come back with you?"

"No, he didn't. He was a little upset when he got word his son had led a raid not too far from here, taken a captive, and when the chiefs wanted to trade for her, he found out the woman had hung herself! I think he was goin' to hunt up his son and try to get him to come to the peace table with the others."

"Did all the other chiefs come back with you?" asked Reuben.

"No, just the Cheyenne including Bull Bear, leader of the Dog Soldiers. Oh, and Left Hand was sick, so he sent his brother, Neva, and three others, Bosse, Knock Knee, and Heap of Buffalo. Wynkoop said they'd be leavin' for Denver City in the mornin'."

"What about the captives?" queried Reuben, frowning.

"Yeah, they got all they could. A young woman name of Laura Roper, and three young uns'."

Reuben nodded, "That's somethin' I guess."

"Ummhmmm," replied Bent, sipping on the hot coffee. He looked up at Reuben and asked, "Uh, we passed the carcass of what looked like a Kiowa, up yonder by that little creek. You wouldn't know anything about that, would you?" he lifted one eyebrow high as he peered over the rim of his cup at Reuben.

"Dunno. Somethin' came screamin' at me outta the dark long 'bout there. Had a big knife in one hand, a tomahawk in the other, and was screamin' so loud I didn't think he wanted to talk trade, so I thought it best just to shoot him. Too dark to dig a grave and I was anxious to get home to Elly, so..." he explained as he shrugged and sipped at his hot coffee.

Bent dropped his eyes, shook his head, and chuckled as he remembered the crowd of carrion eaters that were feasting on the carcass. "Some o' them are so mean, his carcass will prob'ly poison the buzzards!"

Elly stepped from the house and came behind Reuben, resting her hands on his shoulders as Reuben asked, "So, with none of the Arapaho joinin' in with Black Kettle, you think that might be a problem?"

Bent took a deep breath that lifted his shoulders and he turned to look at Reuben. "I honestly don't know. Usually, you can't hardly separate the Cheyenne and the Arapaho, they intermarry and all, but with Little Raven goin' his own way, you'd prob'ly have a better idea of what he's thinkin' than I do."

———

THE NEXT MORNING, BOTH BENT AND REUBEN SAT ON THE porch, watching the band of peace makers ride from the fort. In the lead was Major Wynkoop and Captain Soule, followed by the freed captives and Lieutenant Cramer beside the seven chiefs, led by Black Kettle. A troop of forty soldiers made up the rest of the column with two wagons carrying supplies for the almost weeklong trip to Denver City. Bent raised his steaming cup of coffee high, "Here's to ya' Major. We're hopin' for the best!"

"Amen!" added Reuben, lifting his cup in the ancient salute.

As they watched, a lone rider came from the river crossing and rode up to the stockade. Bent recognized him as John Smith, the crooked trader that had worked with Agent Colley to cheat the Indians of their annuities. But Bent had done business with the trader for many years before the upheaval among the Indians and he welcomed the man to his compound. "C'mon up an' sit in the shade. We've got fresh coffee if'n you're thirsty."

As the three men sat looking out at the bosque and the entourage riding away in the distance, Smith spoke up, "Word came down ol' General Curtis wasn't doin' too good huntin' Indians over Nebraska way, heard about the confederates under ol' "Pap" Price were on the move in Missouri, so Curtis decided to get in the mix and headed back to Fort Leavenworth!"

"Hear anything else 'bout the war?" asked Bent. News of the war was often slow in coming to the west, but occasionally a message came by the telegraph and was quickly passed around.

Smith chuckled, sipped his coffee, and answered, "Most o' the Injun troubles are in Kansas and Nebraska, so Chivington's 3rd regiment ain't been gettin' in on the fight. What with him n' Evans both wantin' to get into politics, their opponents are callin' that bunch the Bloodless 3rd, and sayin' they's just doin' what they is to get statehood and get them into congress!" He shook his head, "Don't make no sense a'tall, why would anybody in they right mind wanna be among all them politicians! They all's a bunch a liars an' thieves!"

Bent shook his head, "Ain't that the pot callin' the kettle black?"

"Now, hol' on just a minute! I ain't no liar an' thief like them fellas!"

"What do you call what you'n Colley been doin' to the Cheyenne and Arapaho?" asked Bent.

"That's different! They's Injuns! Ain't like lyin' to a white man!"

Bent glanced at Reuben, both men shaking their heads, contempt showing on their faces for the man that sat with them. What he and the agent Colley had done was as much a cause for the Indian wars as anything done by the settlers and gold hunters, for their actions were a direct breach of the tenets of the treaty.

"What else have you heard?" asked Reuben, not sure he wanted to hear anything from the man, but anxious for any news.

Smith chuckled again, "Seems a Lieutenant Shoup was promoted to Colonel and given command of the 3rd regiment under Chivington. Course, ever'body knows it's cuz he was shinin' up to Chivington and the governor. And ol' Gen'l Blunt oe'r in Kansas been huntin' some Injuns and can't find 'em, but tween you'n me, he won't be happy if 'n when he does!" He paused, sipped his coffee, and continued, "Course them Dog so'jers and Sioux are still pickin' fights up north on the Overland trail, makin' folks in Denver nervous."

Bent looked at Reuben, "Ain't that the Nebraska 1st Regiment that's doin' the fightin' up on Plum Creek and such?"

Reuben nodded, "I think it is, but the way they been movin' around, changin' officers and so many wantin' to get in the war back east, there's no tellin' from one month to the next."

"Ain't that the truth," answered Bent.

Elly had returned to the house, leaving the men alone on the porch for their talk and needing to have another change of her wound dressing. The wound was mending, and Island had done an exceptional job of tending to the wound and Elly sat down on the edge of the bed as Island came in with fresh bandages and a basin of water and a rag to wash the wound. As she removed the dressing, she looked at the wound, nodded to Elly, "It is healing well, this might be the last bandage." She quickly washed the wound, added the salve to the bandage and applied it as before. She glanced at Elly, "Are the men still talking?"

Elly smiled and laughed, "Don't they always?"

Island said, "Bent likes to hear his own voice. He would make a good chief. But I am tired. I will probably return to my people soon."

Elly frowned, "Why?"

"He wants to go away to his home far to the east. I do not want to leave my land and my people."

"Will he leave soon?"

"Before the snows come," answered Island. "My sister left with her son and is with my people. I will join her. He will find another woman. It is his way."

Elly nodded, understanding the strong tie to family. She knew Island was not Bent's first choice as a wife, but was the sister of his first wife, Owl Woman, who had died. Island stayed to care for the children, but they were older now and had little need of a hovering mother. Elly glanced at Island, saw no sign of sorrow, and realized their relationship was one of need and convenience, but Island wanted to be with her people. Elly understood, thought of Reuben, and knew she was loved and wanted. She thought of her loving husband and smiled, content.

Bent looked over at a rather pensive Reuben and asked, "So, what's got you so quiet all of a sudden?"

Reuben lifted his eyes to Bent, glanced at Smith, and began, "Just thinkin' 'bout those attacks by the Dog Soldiers and Sioux." He leaned forward, elbows on his knees, "I was picturing the lay of the land." He paused, looked at Bent and continued, "In the north, on the Platte River Road, or Overland Trail as some call it, is where many of the attacks have happened, right?"

"Ummhmm," replied Bent, frowning, and leaning forward which prompted Smith to do the same.

"Now, you said the Dog Soldiers and Sioux have been raiding along the Platte, but over in Nebraska and Kansas territory, and the boys in blue haven't had much luck chasin' 'em down. Now, am I right in assuming that after the attacks, the troopers have chased them west toward Colorado territory?" Reuben looked at Smith, waiting for an answer. The trader frowned, and nodded, trying to understand what Reuben was implying.

"And the reports we've gotten about attacks toward Fort Larned have been much the same. The Dog Soldiers and Sioux attack, and run to the west and have always escaped, or most always." He looked at the two frowning men and continued. "Let's go down there," nodding to the compound, "and I'll draw a map in the dirt."

The three men rose and Bent and Smith followed Reuben down the steps. Reuben bent and picked up a stick, walked to a patch of dirt and dropped to one knee. Using the stick, he smoothed out the area and began to draw, explaining as he sketched. "Now here," making a long line at a slight diagonal up and to the right, "is the Platte." He made two similar lines below the first and said, "This is the Arikaree River, and this one is the Republican," both lines sort of paralleling the first but with the second spaced further away from the first. He drew another line that ran level from left to right, "And this is the Arkansas." He jabbed three dots deep in the dirt, one on the Arkansas to indicate Fort Lyon, one further east and above the Arkansas to indicate Fort Larned, and one near the Platte River to indicate Fort Kearny. Then he drew a line from top to bottom, intersecting each of the rivers.

Reuben stood and pointed at his map, "The attacks have mostly been to the east of the territory line, but when they attack, they flee to the west and I'm thinkin' they come into Colorado territory, probably along one of those two rivers between the Platte and the Arkansas. There're probably good hiding places along those rivers, sites for camps and such, and they're far enough away from the forts that the troopers won't follow. Then when things settle down, they go east, find a target and strike, and return, safe and sound."

Bent and Smith frowned, looking at the sketch in the dirt, and Bent looked at Reuben, "You could be right. And that's far enough away from Fort Lyon that the boys here won't go that far, and it's far enough away from Denver City that Chivington and his boys won't come, and likewise from the forts in Nebraska and Kansas territories."

The men looked at the map, pondering what had been said, and Bent was the first to move, "I'm gonna hafta have some fresh coffee to think about that," and turned back to mount the steps and resume his seat on the porch out of the sun. Reuben and Smith followed as Bent hollered for Island to bring them some more coffee.

Elly brought out the coffee and refilled the men's cups. When she stood beside Reuben, she asked, "Did you get everything figured out?"

Reuben chuckled, "I was just showin' 'em what I thought was the tactic of the raiders; how they strike and run, coming back into Colorado territory to hide out until they want to strike again."

Elly frowned, looking at her man, and asked, "Is that what you think?"

"Ummhmmm," replied Reuben, grinning.

"And what are you planning... I can tell by that glint in your eyes?"

"Maybe takin' a ride up that way, see if we can find their camps, maybe try to talk peace."

"Not without me! I've had enough of loafin' around the house. I'm not cut out for that!" declared a grinning Elly.

"Well, maybe we'll just go for a ride, come mornin'."

———

THE SUNRISE LOOKED AS IF THE WORLD HAD BEEN TURNED upside down and all the molten gold was pouring out to fill up the clouds. The brilliant colors of the morning painted the rolling hills, the vast grassy prairie, and the jagged scars of the river bottoms. Even the shoulders and flanks of the horses had a pale gold cast as Reuben aboard his blue roan, and Elly, atop the leopard appaloosa, followed the dim trail north across the flats. Late morning saw them ride the rolling alkali hills that shed their rainwater into the dry creek beds that cut through the rolling hills. It was a barren land, with the only semblance of vegetation, other than cacti, were dead carcasses long greyed by the elements and did little to resemble the once majestic cottonwood sentinels that had marked the land. By unspoken agreement, they pushed on to Sand Creek where willows and scrub cottonwood and alder could provide a bit of shelter from the blazing sun and water was plentiful to refresh the horses.

Reuben reined up at a spot near the backwater of the small creek where the dog-leg bend in the creek had washed away at the bank until the small pool of backwater lay inviting in the shade of a cluster of cottonwoods. He took the reins of the appaloosa, helped Elly to the ground, and led the horses and the pack mule to the water.

"You want some coffee?" called Elly, gathering an armload of branches for firewood.

"Sure! That'd be good," answered Reuben as he loosened the girths on the animals while they dropped their noses into the water.

Elly gathered the wood, built the fire and as the thin tendril of smoke rose to be dissipated among the leaves of the cottonwood, and readied the coffee pot with water from the canteens. The water in the creek was runoff from a rainstorm the night before a little further north and Elly knew it was not suitable for drinking, especially from a creek that split alkali land on its way downstream. Reuben had tethered the animals, stripped the packs from the mule, and gear from the horses, and walked to the fire. The site had been used before and the big grey log lay near the fire ring. He sat down, stretched his legs toward the fire, and looked at Elly as she was busy gathering the left-over biscuits and pork belly to make an offering for their mid-day meal.

Reuben said, "I think we'll rest a mite here, enjoy the shade instead of the hot sun on our faces. What'chu think?"

"Suits me! I was too excited about getting back on the trail to get much sleep last night, so a nap would be nice."

Reuben grinned, enjoying the presence of his wife, and watched her finish her preparations. She handed him a pork sandwich and grabbed his free hand as they bowed their heads to offer their thanks to the Lord. At the "Amen," Elly squeezed Reuben's hand and scooted close beside him to lean her head on his shoulder.

"So, just what do you expect or hope to do if we meet up with these Dog Soldiers?"

"Dunno. Not sure I want to meet up with 'em. If you remember, the last time we did was when they were goin' after that stage, and we had to kill a few. They're mighty good warriors and unless the situation is very much in our favor, we might just have to lay low and avoid 'em."

Elly looked at Reuben, contemplating what he had said and wondering what they might do, then dropped her eyes and finished her biscuit. She rubbed the big dog Bear behind his ears and reached for a cup for some coffee, "Well, while you figure it out, I'm gonna have some coffee, then I'm spreadin' a blanket in the shade and take a nice long nap!"

Reuben chuckled, "You go right ahead. Bear and I will probably go up on that little knoll yonder and have a looksee at our territory."

Elly smiled, knowing the way of her man, and went to the packs for a blanket. She rolled it out in the shade, blew a kiss to Reuben, and stretched out to make herself comfortable. Reuben watched her, finished his coffee, and went to the gear to fetch his Sharps and the binoculars for his survey of the countryside.

25 / IRISH

Just shy of mid-afternoon, Reuben and Elly resumed their journey. With the afternoon sun now off their left shoulder, a slight breeze rippled the tall bunch grass making the flats appear as the wave covered surface of an off-colored lake. Yet the grass was interspersed with patches of cholla and prickly pear cacti, sage and greasewood that rose shoulder high to Reuben's tall roan, and the many trails of predator and prey that wound through the maze. Reuben frowned as he saw Bear sniffing about, looking from the ground, and lifting his head to look in the distance. When the big dog turned back to look at them, it was that expression that told of suspicion and confusion. Reuben moved close behind Bear, stepped down and looked at the trail to see fresh tracks of a shod horse, but bigger tracks than what would usually be found here away from the wagon roads. These were of a horse that was the size of a large draft animal, one used to pull wagons, plows, or freighters. He frowned as he touched the track, seeing the turned soil that was still slightly moist indicating it was less than an hour old. He stood, shaded his eyes as he looked to the distance in the direction the tracks indicated, but there was no sign of a rider.

"What is it?" asked Elly as she nudged her appy near Blue.

Reuben pointed at the ground, "Tracks of a draft horse, or somethin'. But it's only one and the way it's movin' somebody's riding it."

"A draft horse?" asked Elly, frowning and leaning down to look. "It's big, that's for sure! But a plow horse, out here?"

"Ummhmmm. Could be somebody left a wagon train, or somethin' like that. There's no tracks from a wagon or anything, and the way it's moving, it's being ridden." He still stared into the distance, searching for movement or dust, but saw nothing. He looked back at Elly as he stepped back aboard Blue, "I think we'll follow his trail a ways, somethin's not right about this, I've got a funny feeling about it."

Elly slowly lifted her head, looking at Reuben, knowing his *feelings* and how often those feelings had revealed several mysteries and dangers to them. But she also knew there was no way of persuading him to do anything different, not that she wanted to, but sometimes these detours got them into prickly situations. She chuckled to herself and dug heels to her appy to stay close behind Reuben and the pack mule.

The tracks bore to the northeast and the rider was staying well ahead of Reuben and Elly. Although going in basically the same direction that Reuben had planned, he was surprised a lone rider would be traveling in this country, the land of the Arapaho and Cheyenne. It was but a short while after they took to the trail, that the big horse began to follow the sign of a bigger bunch of riders and Reuben guessed this to be the trail of a war party, probably Cheyenne Dog Soldiers, or the war party of the younger Little Raven. He stopped, leaning down to look at the sign, and shook his head, frowning and turned to Elly, "It looks like this rider is trailing the war party, and he's not too far behind. Hope he's smart enough to keep out of sight cuz if they see him, they'll turn back on him, and he won't have a chance!" He shook his head, "Prob'ly some sod buster that ain't never been in Indian country! Looks like he's itchin' to get his scalp lifted!" declared Reuben, disgusted at the presumptive attitude of so many immigrants from the east.

They had been pushing their horses hard, trying to catch up to the rider on the big horse, and the sun was lowering in the west. Lances of gold, orange and pink pierced the blue of the late afternoon sky, casting a pale glow on the flats when Reuben reined up and stood in his stirrups. Frowning, he cocked his head to the side as people are wont to do when they cannot see what they want, but the only break in the monotony of the featureless land was a slight tuft of green that stood above the sage and greasewood. He turned to Elly, "Looks like there's some trees yonder. If he's smart, he'll hole up for the night while he's got some cover. I don't want to go ridin' up blind on him, so we'll make ourselves known."

Elly nodded, knowing the unwritten law of the land was to announce yourself and ask permission to enter another's camp. The bunch grass was sparse, cacti and sage more abundant, but the vague trail kept to the open areas, and it was wide enough for Elly and Reuben to ride side by side, with the pack mule trailing free rein and close behind or beside Blue as the trail allowed. Within moments they neared the greenery, close enough to make out a thicket of cottonwoods with alders and buck brush around the base. Away from the trees, cattails were thick, and bullfrogs could be heard, marking a sizeable marsh. This was probably a stagnant pond fed by a little spring and seldom deep enough to drain away. White showed to the west edge, marking the shallow end that yielded only alkali.

"Hello the camp! Can we come in?" called Reuben, uncertain if there was anyone among the trees. There had not been the glimmer of a fire, no smoke showed, and no sign of any life.

"Who are you and whaddya want?" came a voice, somewhat strained but clear enough.

"We're friendly, just wanted to make camp ourselves!"

"C'mon but keep your hands in the air!" instructed the voice, coming from the deep shadows.

Reuben squeezed his legs to guide Blue as he led the way, both hands high. Elly came close behind, keeping her hands up with the reins dangling from her left hand. As they came into a small clearing before the tall cotton-woods, Blue stopped, and Daisy came alongside and stopped. The pack mule stayed behind Blue, but the big ears were pointing to the trees as were those of the horses.

"Aw'right. You can be for puttin' 'em down, but dinna touch your weepons!" demanded the voice from the shadows.

Reuben frowned, slowly lowered his hands and placed them one atop the other on the saddle horn, Elly followed suit. Both stared into the darkness and Reuben asked, "Can we get down?"

"Aye, but I have me blunderbuss on ye, so be careful."

Reuben frowned, glanced, and nodded to Elly and they both swung a leg over the rump of their horses and stepped to the ground. Turning to face the source of the voice, Reuben asked, "We'd like to fix some coffee and somethin' to eat. Is it alright if we make a fire?"

"Aye," came the voice as the figure came from the trees, but the first thing Reuben's eyes fell on was the brass barreled weapon held at the hip of the person. With a barrel just over two feet long, and the muzzle flared to slightly larger than a man's palm, the blunderbuss was intimidating. He looked up at the one holding it and as the light began to reveal, he was surprised to see the face of a woman. Red hair cascaded over her shoulders, and framed a light complexion, but freckled face. She was not a small woman but had filled out her clothing in all the right places. With men's britches held up by galluses, a linsey Woolsey shirt rolled up at the cuffs, she was surprisingly attractive. Reuben glanced to Elly who stood open mouthed as she looked at the woman.

"And what be the matter with ye? Have ye ne'er seen a prim Irish lass before?"

Reuben chuckled, looking to Elly and back to the woman, "Uh, you're not quite what we expected. But my name is Reuben and this," motioning toward Elly, "is my wife, Elly."

The woman nodded, "And I be Maggie O'Reilly of County Cork, in Ireland. But me'n mine came 'ere from New York!"

Reuben frowned, looking about the small clearing and seeing no one, he looked at the woman, "But you're alone."

"Aye, but not for long. I'm goin' to fetch me wee one back."

Reuben pointed to the blunderbuss, "Could you point that cannon away, it makes me nervous."

The woman laughed, lowered the muzzle of the blunderbuss, "Aye, 'n I thought you were 'bout to be fixin' some coffee and food, be about it if ye will."

Reuben looked about and started gathering up broken branches and limbs, breaking them to size and began to build a fire in the middle of the clearing. It had been used before and he quickly stacked the wood, drew out his small cylindrical match case and struck a lucifer to get the fire going. As the small flames began to hungrily lick at the sticks, Reuben stepped back and looked at the woman, now seated on a big rock back from the fire circle. "You said you were on your way to fetch your wee one?"

"Aye," she answered, adding nothing.

"I assume you mean a child?"

"My wee lad, me boyo Michael, he's but seven, goin' on eight."

"Where is he?" asked Reuben as he glanced to Elly who was digging in the packs for her makings. He started to the horses to strip the gear and take them to water, glancing back at the woman, waiting for an answer.

"If I knew that, I'd be for gettin' him. But I will soon 'nough," she adamantly declared.

Reuben had already spotted the little trickle of water that came from among the trees and undergrowth, and after stripping the gear from the horses and mule, he led them toward the fresh water. As he stepped into the trees, he spotted the woman's big horse, tethered within reach of the water and grazing on some green grass. The animal lifted his head, ears pricked forward to watch the intruders to his glen. His nostrils flared and a deep rumble came from his chest as he greeted the newcomers. Standing over sixteen hands and weighing over fifteen hundred pounds, the wide chested dapple grey was a fine animal. Reuben lifted his brow as he looked at the big horse, standing between the grey and his animals who were crowding one another for the fresh water in the small pool below the little spring. At a glance, he saw the bridle and blanket, but saw no saddle, just a wide girth. He tethered his animals away from the big grey and returned to the clearing.

Elly had fetched the makings and pot from the pack, handed Reuben the coffee pot, and instructed, "Need some water, mister!" she smiled mischievously as she pushed at his shoulder. He knew it was a move to make him leave, and he took the hint, knowing the women would be more likely to open up to one another without him nearby. He chuckled and disappeared into the trees.

26 / CHASE

They lay together, hands behind their heads and looking at the stars. With a low voice, Elly began to explain what she learned from Maggie. "Their wagons were attacked, her husband killed, her son taken. So, with nowhere to go, she thought it best to try to rescue her boy."

Reuben frowned, turned to look at Elly, "But, weren't there other wagons and people?"

"Their wagon had broken an axle and they were left behind. Her husband was a carpenter and was carving an axle from a burr oak by the river when the Indians came. The boy was helping his father and she was off picking berries. When she came back, the Indians were gone, her husband and one of the horses were dead, the other'n ran off in the trees. She caught up the horse, dug the blunderbuss from the wrecked wagon, which the Indians had tried to burn but it didn't, and mounted up on their last horse and started out after her boy."

"That's crazy!" declared Reuben.

"No, I don't think so, if it'd been me and somebody

had my only child and had killed my man, I'da done the same thing!"

Reuben frowned, looking at Elly who still stared at the stars. He slowly shook his head, trying to understand, reckoned it to be something only a woman and mother could understand, and rolled to his back. Yet as he thought about it, hadn't he done the same thing when the Comanche took Elly? He chuckled to himself and said, "Let's get some sleep. I'm thinkin' you've got plans to help her, am I right?"

Elly giggled quietly, "Ummhmm."

———

"Now look, if you're thinkin' of goin' against any of those Dog Soldiers, you need somethin' better'n that blunderbuss!" declared Reuben, looking at the red headed Irish lass.

Maggie frowned, "And what's wrong with me blunderbuss! It suits me just fine!"

"One shot. That's all you have. So, what're you gonna do about the other fifteen or so warriors that are still standing?"

"Uh, uh, I'll just have to be a chancer," she mumbled.

Reuben frowned, "Forget about what you thought you could do, and let's try to improve the odds in our favor." He paused, turned to pick up the weapon he had taken from the packs and lifted it before him. "This is a Colt revolving shotgun. It holds five rounds or loads." He pointed at the cylinder and continued, "I will show you how to load it, but it will be loaded before you take it. And we'll let you shoot it a couple times to get used to it," offered Reuben. He lay the shotgun across his lap and began instructing her how to take out the cylinder, load each chamber, and when they finished, he lifted the shotgun to his shoulder and began to explain, "Now this is a little different than what you might be used to, you have to hold it a little different."

When he finished showing and telling her about it, they walked to the edge of the clearing, well away from the horses sheltered in the trees, and he lifted the shotgun to his shoulder, pointed to a cluster of sage, and pulled the trigger. The shotgun roared, bucked, and spat smoke and many pellets of lead that shredded the sage-brush. As the roar subsided and he waved away the cloud of smoke, he handed it to Maggie, "Your turn."

The shotgun rocked her back on her heels, but she held on and waved away the smoke to see what damage she had done to the sage. A slow grin split her face as she looked from the sage to Reuben, "It sure be a noisy thing, but it carries a powerful punch!"

Reuben grinned, "It does. Satisfied?"

"Aye, now I need to reload. You watch while I do the deed!" she declared, turning back to the clearing and to the waiting rock and pouch with the makings.

Elly stepped close and watched as Maggie deftly loaded the empty cylinders and did as Reuben instructed, "When you bring the hammer back one notch, that's on safety. But some also remove the cap on that cylinder, just for extra safety."

She looked at the cylinder, removed the cap and put it in the small pouch, nodded and stood. "I must be going!" and started to the horses.

"Uh, hold on there. We'll be going with you, you can use all the help you can get, believe me!" stated Reuben, taking Elly's hand as they walked through the trees to the waiting horses.

———

THEY RODE THROUGH THE MORNING, THE SUN TAKING ITS time rising to its zenith but shared all its warmth and blazing heat as it did. The three riders stayed close to one another, often having to leave the trail of the war party to avoid being seen. In the wide-open flats of the great plains, there is often little cover bigger than sagebrush and they had to take advantage of the low rolling hills and occasional flat topped ridges and plateaus.

"Looks like there's water yonder," suggested Reuben, nodding to the northeast. The terrain was a little more hilly, offering scattered juniper and piñon, blue green sage that grew to the height of Blue's shoulder, and rocky rolling hills. The brighter green of cottonwoods beckoned and Reuben pointed his big roan toward the wide gulley that held the greenery. As they dropped into the gulley, Reuben paused, frowned, and looked at Elly, "You hear that? Sounds like gunfire!"

Elly paused, keeping a taut rein on Daisy, and frowned as she held her breath to listen, "You're right! It is, and with that much, there's got to be a fight!"

"Prob'ly the Dog Soldiers either hittin' a wagon train cuz we're near the Smoky Hill River Road, or maybe a rancher."

"What do you want to do?" asked Elly, looking about at the ravine and the inviting water in the tiny creek.

"I'm gonna let Blue drink, then I'll go ahead, find some place where I can have a look see, and then decide. You two be ready, I might be back and in a hurry!"

Elly swung her leg over the rump of the appy and Maggie bellied down on the big grey and slid to the ground. They led their horses to the trickle of water beside Blue, and Elly looked up at her man, "Are you takin' Bear with you?"

Reuben slowly shook his head, "Nah, he better stay with you. I'll be findin' a place to hide, although there's not much to hide behind and Bear might get a little too excited with all the shootin'. You keep him here with you, a little extra protection for you."

"Then you be careful and make sure you come back to me!" declared Elly, looking up at her man.

"You know I will," answered Reuben, nudging Blue around to take to the low swales and gullies between the low rising hills.

It was but a few moments before the shooting had a lull and Reuben pushed Blue into a little cluster of juniper. He dropped to the ground, Sharps in one hand, the binoculars in the other, and began to slowly pick his way to the crest of the sage and cacti covered knoll. Near the top, a twisted cedar stood beside some boulders, and he bellied down to crawl beside the gnarly tree. Below was a jumbled bunch of wagons, hastily drawn together for protection, that held several shooters that were making a lot of noise but not doing much damage. The Indians had apparently lain in wait, using the rolling terrain and the sage, greasewood, and few piñon trees for cover and had caught the wagon train in their ambush.

Reuben brought his binoculars up, using an overhanging branch to give some shade and prevent a glare from the sun that lay behind him. As he searched the terrain before him, he spotted most of the warriors either by their movements or the gunsmoke. But several were using bows and arrows, launching the feathered shafts in a long arch to drop behind the barriers of the wagons. The warriors were taking their time, picking their shots, and refusing to allow themselves to be seen. But the men of the wagons were getting impatient and were becoming careless, trying to find the Indians and get a shot by exposing themselves and standing on the seats of the wagons or lifting the canvas coverings to give them a better view. As Reuben watched he saw two men take hits, one with an arrow through his throat and when he fell, Reuben could hear the screams of the man's woman.

Reuben scanned the battlefield, saw one of the warriors take a bullet and fall into the sage, but others were well out of sight and the rifles from the wagons were doing little harm. As he moved the binoculars along the line of warriors, he saw most of the men and mentally marked their positions, all would be within range of his Sharps, but he couldn't start shooting yet. Dropping the binoculars, he searched the area for any possible location for the Indians' horses. He spotted a low rise with what appeared to be a long draw behind it, and lifting his field glasses, he saw the movement of horses. With a quick look around, he crabbed back from the crest, moved to the far end of the butte, and taking shelter behind some more rocks, he looked at the draw again. There were all the horses and two young warriors tending the animals. Under the overhang of a nearby juniper, he saw the figure of a boy stretched out in the shade, but with a tether on his ankles and his wrists tied. Reuben nodded to himself and pulled back from the rocks to return to his horse.

———

"HERE'S WHAT WE'LL DO..." BEGAN REUBEN AS HE watched the women mount their horses. He clucked

Blue to step across the little stream and led the way, talking to the women as they moved. Nearing the butte he had used for his lookout, he pointed to the long draw that would take the women behind the low rise and give them access to the draw with the horses. "Now, wait until you hear me start shooting. That way, if you have to shoot, the Dog Soldiers won't be too surprised to hear gunfire behind them." The women nodded and started for the low draw, Elly glancing back to see Reuben move with Blue into the trees and step down. They looked at one another, nodded, and continued.

Once in place, Reuben stretched out with the Sharps, lay out several paper cartridges and caps within easy reach. Behind him lay the Henry, fully loaded and ready if needed. He gave the Sharps scope a last check, then brought the big rifle to his shoulder, earing back the hammer as he picked his target. As he looked, he thought the warriors were getting ready to move and thought to himself *Guess I'll hafta change their mind!* His first target appeared to be a leader that was giving orders and Reuben squeezed off his shot.

Before the roar of the Sharps faded, he had reloaded and was picking another target. He dropped the hammer again, and another warrior fell face first into the sage that had given him cover. Reuben moved back from the tree, taking his second position to the far side of the big rock and picked another target.

Although the warriors were about two hundred yards away, his scope was giving him the advantage for a two-hundred-yard shot was nothing to a sharpshooter that had made many kills from five hundred yards and more. The third time the Sharps roared, more screams and war cries came from the flats beyond. He knew they were confused, probably searching the area behind them within a hundred yards, but nothing came from that close by, but when the Sharps bucked again, one warrior screamed and pointed to the low butte and the rock outcroppings.

Reuben chuckled, knowing he was not in danger from any of the weapons of the Dog Soldiers, and he quickly reloaded for another shot. He saw several of the warriors turn and rise slightly, pointing and shouting his direction, and as four of them started toward him at a run, he carefully took aim and dropped one with a chest shot.

He moved again, knowing that if the warriors came to him, they would search where he had been, giving him time to take more down. When he took his third position, laying the Henry at his side, he saw only one of the three remaining warriors that had charged toward him. He quickly brought the Sharps to bear and squeezed off another kill shot. But as he lowered the Sharps, a rattle of stones to his right warned him, making him turn just in time to see two warriors, one taking aim with a rifle, the other charging with upraised tomahawk. Reuben grabbed up the Henry, eared back the hammer and shot from his hip, taking the rifle bearing warrior in the neck.

Before he could jack another round, the first warrior was upon him, screaming and lifting the tomahawk overhead. Reuben lifted the Henry to block the blow, but the charge of the warrior drove him to the ground. The warrior was lean but muscled and was grabbing for his knife but kept the pressure against Reuben and the Henry with his tomahawk. Reuben struggled, pushing against the weight of the man, seeing the hatred in his black eyes, and hearing his grunts and growls, but Reuben's will gave him strength and he pushed against the man, brought his knee up into the warrior's groin, but felt the cold steel of the Dog Soldier's knife drive into his side. Reuben gave a shove, swung the butt of the Henry at the warrior to drive him away. He used the barrel as a club and smashed down on the man's neck and shoulder, heard the crack of the man's collar bone, saw him wince, and used that second's hesitation to jack a round into the chamber and jam the muzzle under the warrior's chin and pull the trigger. Blood splattered, the warrior fell back and Reuben kicked him away, grabbing at the knife in his side and pulled it free. Blood covered his hand and he grabbed at the shirttail of his linen shirt, tore most of it away and jammed it under his jacket to cover the wound. His breath came in ragged bursts, each one making him wince from his wound, and he frowned, for he heard no shooting.

27 / FRIENDS

"Remember, Reuben said if we stampede the horses, the guards will go after the animals, and we can get your boy. But don't hesitate to shoot if one comes at you!" whispered Elly, looking at Maggie. The redhead sat aboard the big grey and looked down at Elly, forced a smile, "May we both be in Heaven before the devil knows we're dead!" declared Maggie, nodding to her new friend.

"If it's alright with you, I'd just as soon not make that trip today!" answered Elly, chuckling. With a nod, she dug heels into the appy's ribs and the spotted horse plunged ahead, Maggie did the same and the big horse made a great lunge and both women charged into the draw between the two ridges. The lazily grazing horses lifted their heads together, eyes wide, ears pointing, and spun around to take flight away from the monstrous dapple grey that was bigger than any horse they had seen.

The two young warriors who had been seated on rocks on the flank of the rise behind them, jumped to their feet, lifting lances, and screaming their war cry. But the stampeding horses scared them, and one turned to chase after the horses, but the other lifted his lance to fight off the attackers. He hesitated just a moment when he saw the red headed woman atop the big horse and the big black dog that was coming at him, but he cocked back the lance just as the big Colt shotgun roared and the blast of a handful of lead pellets splattered against his chest, ripping it open and driving him to his back. Maggie stared at the young warrior, reining up the big grey, but a cry came from the tree, and she immediately turned to see Elly slip from the appy, and cut the tether and bindings on the youngster's wrists. As Maggie came near, Elly lifted the boy up to his mother who grabbed him in a bear hug, but quickly put him behind her and hollered, "Hold on tight!"

Elly swung back aboard the appaloosa and the two women charged from the draw, returning the way they came. They stopped where they had parted from Reuben, heard the lull in the shooting and Elly stood in her stirrups to search for her man. She spotted movement by some rocks, saw Reuben stand, bend to grab his Henry and his Sharps and start down the hill. Elly frowned as she watched her man, seeing him stumble slightly and she quickly stepped to the ground to run to him. Bear was beside her and Elly caught Reuben as he staggered and missed a step. The two almost crashed down together, but she stood strong and said, "Where you hit?"

"Knife... side," he grunted, wincing at the pain. Elly put his arm around her shoulder and helped him to the trees where the big roan waited.

"Did the Cheyenne leave?" she asked, frowning, and trying to look at his wound.

"Dunno," answered Reuben with a groan.

"We chased off their horses, so they haven't gone far, unless they're chasing their mounts."

"Might notta been such a good idea," answered Reuben, feeling the pain. "Help me up on my horse," he directed, frowning. Once aboard, he watched Elly step back aboard the appy and he said, "The shooting's stopped, so maybe we can make it to the wagons." He looked at Maggie, saw a little face peeking around from behind her, "I see you got'chur young'un!"

"Thanks to you two an' I'm mighty beholden," replied a smiling Maggie, wiping tears from her cheeks.

They rode with rifles across their thighs, searching the brush and sage for any movement, as they made their way toward the wagons. The pack mule, free rein, followed close behind and as they neared, they heard someone shout, "Make way for those riders! They're here to help!"

A man stepped to the front of a wagon, lifted the long tongue, and moved aside a big wooden crate to make a way for them to ride into the middle of the formation of wagons. Reuben led the way into the circle, nodding to the men, "Afternoon folks, looks like you could use a little help!"

Several men crowded near and one man who appeared to be the wagon master said, "Mister, you don't know how glad we was to hear you shootin' from out there! Why when you cut loose, them Injuns turned tail an' skedaddled!" He paused, frowning, "That *was* you, wasn't it?"

Reuben forced a grin, nodding slowly, "It was, but it wasn't just me, my wife and her friend stampeded their horses. When they realized that, they had to take off after 'em. Now, don't go droppin' your guard, they might be back. Those were Cheyenne Dog Soldiers you were fightin' with, and they don't give up too easy."

The wagon master frowned, looking at Reuben and the way he held his side, "Are you hurt?"

Reuben nodded, "Had a little scuffle with one of 'em up on that hillside. He cut me a mite."

The wagon master motioned to several of the men, "You men, help him down, we gotta get him bandaged up— George, you go get my Martha, she's the best we got at that!"

Reuben leaned down to accept the offered help, winced at the pain and groaned as they lifted him to the ground. As his feet touched ground, he nodded to Elly, "If you have some bandages, my wife can patch me up. You best watch for the Cheyenne!"

The wagon master started barking orders, instructing men to return to their places, then turned to Reuben, "You really think they'll be back?"

"The best thing you can do is get these wagons movin' as soon as possible and get as far from here as you can. They will be back, if for nothin' else than to get their dead, and there's a few of 'em out there. But if you're gone, they might just take their losses and leave."

"Then that's what we'll do!" declared the wagon master and started around the wagons, telling everyone to get ready to leave. They would have to hitch up the animals and get lined out, but an experienced train could do that in short order.

The wagon master's wife watched over Elly's shoulder as she accepted the bandages but applied her own salve. The woman asked, "What is that you're using on that wound, missy?" Elly kept working, speaking over her shoulder at the woman, "This is the Balm of Gilead, it's made from the fresh buds of the aspen trees, when they're showing red. It also has some bear grass root and sage. It's been used by the natives for centuries."

"And they called it the Balm of Gilead? That's from the Bible!"

"No, it was the black robes, early priests and missionaries that gave it that name," explained Elly, finishing the bandage. She stood, looking around for Maggie and saw her talking with another woman, her son playing with another boy nearby. Elly turned to help Reuben to his feet, and nodded toward Maggie, "Looks like she's found a friend."

Martha looked where they were looking, saw the two women, "That lady just lost her man in the fight, looks like your friend is giving her some comfort."

"Would there be room for her on the train?" asked Reuben.

"Prob'ly, why?"

"She just lost her husband a few days ago in another attack by these same Cheyenne. She came here to rescue her son from them and he's all she has left," explained Reuben.

"Now, she might just be what Esther needs, someone who understands and helps her with her two young'uns. I'll talk to my husband, I'm sure we can take her with us," she paused, turned back to Reuben, and asked, "She doesn't have anything?"

Reuben shook his head, grinned, "Her son, that big horse, and a blunderbuss."

The woman grinned, shaking her head, and started off to find her man.

———

THE SUN WAS CRADLED IN THE WESTERN HILLS AS THE wagons pushed into the fading light. Reuben and Elly watched from atop a low rise south of the wagon road and stood in their stirrups to wave at the distant woman atop the big horse. Elly smiled, "That was a short friendship, but I sure am glad we could help her get her boy back."

"Ummhmm," answered Reuben. "But now, we need to put some miles between us and wherever those Dog Soldiers are, and I'm hopin' they're still headin' northeast, cuz we're goin' south."

"South? What happened to the search for the camps of the raiders, the Dog Soldiers, and the Sioux and maybe the younger Little Raven's bunch?"

"After that fight, I don't care where they are, as long as we're not in the same country. I thought about maybe tryin' to find Little Raven's camp and see if they're gonna be part of the peace treaty."

Elly nodded, smiling, "I'm with you! And don't forget it!" she giggled as she slapped legs to the appaloosa to get a head start on her man. She called over her shoulder, "The last one that finds a camp has to cook supper!"

28 / DENVER

"You said it right!" declared Governor Evans, speaking over his shoulder to Colonel Chivington as he watched out the window of his office wanting to see the entourage of Indian chiefs led by Major Wynkoop leave to return to their villages.

"The Major overstepped his authority even bringing them here! If it had been me, I would've killed them all!" responded Chivington.

"That impudent bunch of savages had some gall coming into my office and telling me what we should do! If word gets out about this, and it will, it could ruin our political aspirations!" fumed Evans, turning back to his desk and dropping into his chair. He shook his finger at Chivington, "You best get the 3rd Regiment up to force and quickly, that's the only way we can do as promised and end this confounded Indian uprising! I want every blasted one of them heathen redskins dead! I said it before and I'll say it again, every citizen of Colorado should go in pursuit of all hostiles and kill and destroy them as enemies of the country!" He continued shaking

190

his finger at the military man and chastising him, "Now, what do you propose?"

"We're not up to force yet, but I have Captain Nichols keeping scouts out and we hope to soon have a crack at the raiding parties near the Overland Trail. According to what they," nodding toward the window to indicate the chiefs that had just left, "said, those that are raiding out there are the Dog Soldiers and Sioux. As soon as we're up to strength, and that'll be soon, I plan to start moving south toward Fort Lyon. In the meantime, I've got a good man to replace Wynkoop, Major Scott Anthony, who believes as we do about the extermination of all Indians."

"Will the 3rd Regiment be enough?" asked the governor.

"I believe I can commandeer some additional companies from the 1st Regiment, and when ready, we'll have the entire force from Fort Lyon. Should number about six or seven hundred troops!" declared a smug Chivington.

"But the last report from Blunt said the Cheyenne and Arapaho number about fifteen hundred warriors!" implored Evans, concerned.

"But we will have artillery and the element of surprise. Even with less, we can still destroy all of them!" assured Chivington.

"Then get to it! I've got some politickin' to do, some concerned citizens to reassure and I'll be telling them that you are going to settle this Indian issue, once and for all!" He leaned forward, his elbow on his desk and shook his finger at the Colonel, "And don't make a liar out of me! If you succeed and everything else falls in place, we'll usher in Colorado as a state, and the two of us will be the first senator and representative for

Colorado in Washington! We have a lot at stake, don't fail!" The Colonel grinned, stood, and turned on his heel to exit the office and put his plan in place. He could smell the gunpowder and blood already.

———

THEY STOPPED ATOP THE SLIGHT RISE THAT OVERLOOKED the meandering creek and all its greenery. Just beyond the creek rose the many lodges of the Arapaho under Little Raven and Reuben grinned, looked at Elly, "Ready to go see our friends?"

"I am!" she declared, nodding to the village below.

As they neared the camp, word quickly spread, and they were recognized. Several women were busy at the edge of the camp scraping hides and one stood, shaded her eyes, and when she recognized the visitors, she dropped her scraper and ran towards Elly. "Yellow Bird! Yellow Bird!"

Elly saw the young woman running toward her, heard her call, and recognized Wind in Her Hair. Elly slid to the ground and welcomed Wind with open arms. The women rejoiced as Red Bear and Running Antelope also joined them and they chattered among themselves, walking together into the camp.

The center of the camp held a compound that offered space for dances, drums and a large cookfire, but only small cookfires smoked among the many lodges. One hide tipi, a little larger than most and painted with the emblem of Little Raven, lay on the west edge of the compound, it's entry facing to the east and the rising sun. Little Raven stood beside the lodge, his usual stoic expression and stately stance, arms folded across his chest, three feathers fluttering in the breeze at the topknot at the back of his head. The hair pipe bone breast plate hung over his broad chest, rippling shoulders protruding to the side and muscled upper arms brandishing silver bands. The fringe on his leggings stirred with each movement, and the sun shone on the intricate beadwork on the breechcloth and moccasins. As Reuben looked at the chief, he was again impressed with the regal bearing of the well-respected chief.

As Reuben neared, a slight smile tugged at the corners of the chief's mouth, and he nodded, "Reuben, my friend. It is good to see you again, and so soon. What brings you to our village this time?"

Reuben chuckled, extending his hand to shake with the chief, "We were coming from the Smoky Hill River Road where we encountered some of the Dog Soldiers. Thought we would stop in and see how the peace negotiations were coming along."

The chief dropped his eyes, motioned to the willow back rests beside the lodge and as the men seated themselves, "I do not know, I have not heard."

"You have not heard? Did you not go with the other chiefs to see the governor?"

"No, I came back to my village after we had our peace conference. Black Kettle and others agreed to go see the white chief."

Reuben looked at his friend, noticed a touch of hesitancy, and asked, "What is it, my friend, why didn't you go with the others?"

Little Raven looked at Reuben, down at the ground and back at his friend, "There are those that choose to fight and do not want this peace. I thought I might do more for peace if I kept the others from attacking the soldiers that took the chiefs to the city."

Reuben caught the glint of sorrow in the chief's eye and asked, "Your son?"

Little Raven nodded, "And others. Was it Tall Bull that you fought with by the Smoky Hill River Road?"

"I think so, but I don't know for sure. I have never met Tall Bull. They were attacking a wagon train on the road, but before that they had attacked a lone wagon down by the Arkansas, killed a man and took his boy. We met the boy's mother, she was on her way after the Dog Soldiers, determined to get her boy back, so, we helped her."

Little Raven looked up at Reuben, "Did you kill any of Tall Bull's warriors?"

"They were attacking the wagon train, and they had the boy, so, yeah, we killed some, but we got the captive back and the wagon train left, so..." he shrugged and leaned back against the willow back rest. He looked at Little Raven, "Do you plan to make peace with the white governor and the soldiers?"

"My people want an end to fighting, and we must have peace. There are too many settlers, and the buffalo are few. We have not seen many this season, and it does not look as if there will be enough for our winter. We must have the rations as promised by the white man. We are on the land of what they call the reservation, but they want to take much of it away, again. And they do not give the rations and other goods as promised. If we do not get them, my people will go hungry in the time of snows."

"So, what do you plan to do?"

"We will do what they ask, but I do not trust them. Every treaty we have signed had many promises, and now the reservation is made smaller again. We will do as they say, but I will not trust them. They want to take our weapons so we cannot fight, but we cannot hunt, and we will go hungry. If we do not, they will send more soldiers like the soldiers that make war against us. I have heard of the attacks by the big general called Blunt who took his many soldiers to fight the *Heévâhetaneo'o* and the *Hinonó eino*. Our people, the Cheyenne and Arapaho, had almost one hundred people killed, not all were warriors. They killed women and children also. That battle was near your Fort Larned, east from here by many days." He paused, looked at Reuben and shook his head, "That was after the chiefs went with Wynkoop to see the governor."

Reuben shook his head, tired of the hypocrisy of the white soldiers and the politicians, none of whom cared anything about the native people, and none seemed to think it necessary to keep their word when they made out the treaties and demanded the native people give up their homeland and go to a reservation, usually in some desolate location on property that no white man would want. He looked at Little Raven, "Well my friend, I hope you know that if I could do something about it, I would. But I do agree with you. Whatever comes, don't be in a hurry to trust what they, the soldiers, and agents, say or promise. Always keep your people safe and in a place where they can feed themselves."

Reuben shifted his position to get a little more comfortable and winced as he twisted around. Little Raven frowned, noticed the dried blood at his side, "Did you get hurt in the fight with the Dog Soldiers?"

Reuben forced a grin, twisting a little more for comfort, and answered, "I did have a little scuffle with one. He stuck his knife in my side, but Yellow Bird tended it and it will heal."

"What did you do to the other?"

"Left him."

Little Raven understood what Reuben meant and nodded his head in understanding. He knew his friend was a formidable warrior and would not be easy to kill. "You will stay with us?"

"For a day or two. I'd like to get back to the fort, see what happened with the peace journey," answered Reuben, leaning back again as he watched Elly and the other women come near to begin their preparations for the evening meal. He knew they would be welcome, and the chief would provide them with a lodge for as long as they needed, but he was anxious to get back to the fort and they would probably travel soon.

29 / REPORT

The slow setting sun painted the western sky with its last daub of color and slowly wrapped itself in the cloak of darkness, sending notice to the heavenly bodies to light their lanterns for the night. The coolness of the night settled about the stockade of William Bent as Reuben and Elly made themselves comfortable in one of the hide lodges just outside the wall. Bear lay down next to Elly, his head on his paws as he looked at the blonde-haired woman, waiting for her attention and her usual caresses before sleep. As she rubbed his scruff behind his ears, he thumped his tail on the blanket to show his appreciation and pushed himself even closer.

"Sometimes I think you love that dog more'n me!" chuckled Reuben, reaching across Elly to add his strokes of affection to the big dog.

"Well, I do believe he loves me just as much as you do, maybe more!" declared Elly, letting a bit of a giggle escape.

"Nope, he can't! Ain't nobody or no thing ever loved another as much as I love you!"

She rolled over to face her man, cradling his face in her hands, and kissed him fervently.

———

THERE WAS JUST A HINT OF GREY IN THE EASTERN SKY when Reuben pushed back the flap of the tipi and stepped out into the crisp morning air. Bear moved beside him, leaning against Reuben's leg to let him know he was near. With his Sharps in hand, the binoculars in the case that hung from his shoulder, Reuben started for the crest of the low rise behind the stockade. It was just a short walk to the top and Bent had built a small bench for a place of rest. The knoll overlooked the bosque at the confluence of the Purgatoire and Arkansas rivers, and to the grounds of Fort Lyon just beyond. Behind him and in all four directions of the compass, stretched the flats and rolling hills of the prairie.

The slow rising sun was beginning to paint the eastern sky in muted grey, pushing aside the dark blue of the night and readying the world for the usual splash of color that would herald the new day. As Reuben twisted on his seat, he saw the entire canopy of the sky was crowded with clouds, some even showing dark bellies that suggested a foreboding sign of weather. The breeze had fallen off and the air was still, but a chill lingered in the air that caused Reuben to shiver, making him frown at the thought of the coming fall. In the mountains, it was easy to see the announcements of the season of colors where aspen decked the mountains with gold and buck brush added splashes of red.

Reuben flipped open the Bible and began to read in Luke 23, *Then shall they begin to say to the mountains, Fall on us; and the hills, Cover us.* He knew the scripture referenced the time when Jesus would be crucified, but it was also a warning of the evil of the time, and he thought of all the death and turmoil that filled the land about him; the war in the east where brother fought against brother, father against son, and the Indian wars here in the great plains where the many native tribes fought for their homes and way of life and greedy politicians thought only of themselves. He shook his head and looked Heavenward, *Lord, I know you know what's goin' on, but it sure would be nice if you give us some direction down here.*

Reuben took a deep breath, looked to the colors beginning in the east and lifted the binoculars from the case to begin his customary scan of the territory. As he looked, he thought of what Bent had told him about the peace conference. The chiefs had proposed a peace, but the governor and Chivington ordered them, as a show of their commitment to peace, to bring their people in to Fort Lyon and make their peace with Wynkoop. He remembered Bent saying, "And then that two-faced Chivington picked one of his popinjay yes boys as a replacement for Wynkoop, a Major Scott Anthony who believes just like Chivington and thinks the only way to have peace with the natives is to kill 'em all! And he does that just when Wynkoop has all the chiefs believin' in him and they're all on their way to the fort!" Of course, Bent said a few other things after that, but Reuben just grinned at the remembrance as he scanned the flats north and east of the fort.

With nothing in sight in the pale light of early morning, Reuben leaned back to have his time in prayer and a little more reading. Yet it was but a few moments later that he saw movement in the distance to the northeast of the fort, and more movement directly north. The small group to the north appeared to be soldiers, a contingent of about a dozen, riding direct to the fort, but the dust in the northeast was from a much larger group. Reuben lingered a while, watching the larger group and guessed that to be some of the natives coming to the fort as they had been ordered, but what band or village he could not tell. With a last scan around, he put the field glasses away and with rifle in hand, started back toward Bent's home and the stockade.

Reuben was surprised to see William Bent sitting on the porch, a steaming cup of coffee in his hand as he watched Reuben come into the compound. With a nod, he looked past Reuben. From his seat on the porch, it was easy to see over the stockade walls to the fort beyond, and his eyes settled on the band of natives approaching the fort. Reuben mounted the steps and turned to look, "Looks like some of the Cheyenne or Arapaho comin' in like they said," suggested Reuben.

"Yeah, reckon so. Hate to see it cuz I don't think they'll get a fair shake. I think the other bunch was the new commandant for the fort."

"What'd you say his name was, Anthony?" asked Reuben, seating himself on the long bench near Bent's chair. At the sound of the men talking, Elly came out, smiled at Reuben, and mouthed the word, "Coffee?" Reuben nodded and looked back at Bent.

"Yeah, Major Scott Anthony, a Chivington protégé," moaned Bent, his disgust obvious.

Reuben frowned as he looked at Bent, surprised at his use of the term, protégé, which was a bit unusual for the man Reuben had become used to using very simplistic yet descriptive language, sometime even coarse, but nothing quite like his spitting the term protégé. "I never expected to hear that word from you, Bent," chuckled Reuben as he sipped his hot coffee.

"Yeah, I heard it somewhere, seemed to fit the pair!" growled Bent.

Reuben nodded toward the dust beyond the fort, "Who do you reckon that is?"

"Prob'ly Black Kettle, he's been leadin' all along, so I'm guessin' he'll bring his people in first, then maybe Left Hand and Little Raven."

"When we talked with Little Raven, he wasn't ready to trust Wynkoop."

"It ain't Wynkoop that's the problem, it's those generals and politicians pullin' the strings!"

———

"ENTER!" RESPONDED MAJOR WYNKOOP AT THE KNOCK ON his office door.

A tousle headed corporal came in, eyes downcast, "There's a Major Anthony to see you sir!"

"Show him in, Corporal."

The corporal had no sooner cleared the doorway than a big man stepped through to stand before the desk of Wynkoop. The man was broad-shouldered, standing over six feet tall, broad forehead over a single brow, and lantern jawed. His uniform was dusty but orderly and his hat was under his left arm as he clapped heels together and snapped a salute. "Major Scott Anthony reporting to assume command of the fort sir!"

Wynkoop looked at the man, intentionally pausing before returning the salute and finally did, slowly standing, "Major! Good to see you made it safe. Have you been shown your quarters yet?"

"Uh, no," replied Anthony, looking at Wynkoop and around the office, showing himself to be a little uncomfortable, and seating himself. Wynkoop returned to his seat and leaned his elbows on his desk to look at his replacement.

"Then I'll be gathering my things together and turn everything over to you by the end of the day."

"Uh, there's no rush, major. I would prefer you stay on for a few weeks or so to help acquaint me with the situation. I'm not familiar with these Indians and it would be good to know more about them," suggested Anthony.

"The situation is this—the Indians want peace, the same peace that was offered to them along with annuities and rations and the reservation, but the Governor and Commissioner of Indian Affairs seems to think it would be better to kill them all! And that sentiment is echoed by Colonel Chivington, and probably General Curtis as well. But the Governor and Chivington said the chiefs could make their peace with me and stay here at Fort Lyon. So, as we speak, those same tribes are on their way here to make their winter camp and to receive the promised annuities that were guaranteed them by the provisions of the last two treaties!"

"I have been ordered to cease and desist any and all distribution of annuities or rations!"

Wynkoop shook his head, "Major Anthony, the government of this nation had promised these people annuities and rations and a significant amount of money in payment for all the land you crossed to get here! Their reservation stretched from the Arkansas River," nodding toward the river behind him and visible from his office window, "to the Platte River, from the Rocky Mountains into the Kansas Territory!" He stood to his feet and leaned forward on the desk to put his face near that of Anthony who leaned back in his chair, "Instead, they have had all this land taken from them, did not receive the promised payment, nor the annuities and rations, and still the idiots in charge in the army and the government think the problem is with the Indians!"

Major Anthony stood to his feet, stepped away from the chair and cocked one eyebrow as he looked down at Major Wynkoop, "It's easy to see who the Indian lover is in this post!" snarled the bigger man.

"On the contrary! It is easy to see who believes we, as representatives of the government, should have some integrity and character and live up to our part of the agreement! All these people, who approached us with the desire for peace, want is what is properly owed them. These rations are necessary for them to live through the winter. Where there were vast herds of buffalo that provided for these people, there are now wagon roads, broken wagons, prospect holes, and settlers trying to turn a prairie into farmland." Wynkoop stood, turned away from the newcomer and looked out the window. He turned back to face Anthony, "And before this day is over, there will be about six to seven hundred natives, over half of them proven warriors, just outside this fort. You have less than one hundred soldiers to defend this fort. You must decide to either feed the natives or try to subdue them with your one hundred soldiers. Oh, and before this week is over, there will be over one thousand warriors!"

30 / REPLACEMENT

"My orders are to go to Fort Riley, but Major Anthony said he wanted me to stick around a while longer, help him get acquainted with the Cheyenne and Arapaho. But I'm not too sure he wanted to get acquainted, it's a matter of record that he agrees with Chivington and thinks there should be a major war of extermination against all Indians, he just wants to control them until that happens," declared Major Wynkoop as he sat on Bent's porch.

"What about Captain Soule, is he getting along with Anthony?" asked Bent.

"Both he and Lieutenant Cramer are doing all they can, but they're not happy about the way Anthony is going back on everything we agreed upon with the governor and promises we made about giving out the annuities and rations. They don't know that I know, but they've been soliciting signatures for a letter of commendation for me from the officers and another from families throughout the valley hereabouts. But there's little else they can do. I'll be leaving soon but I'm hoping Anthony will at least *try* to keep things in order.

I'm hoping to make headway with General Curtis and get the treaty solidified before everything falls apart."

"I'm not sure what it is, but it just seems to me there is something else going on behind closed doors. After what was reported on the council in Denver, and the way things have been happening in other parts of the territory, I dunno, I just can't shake the feeling that things are going to blow up soon!" declared Reuben, squirming a little on his seat as the men held out their cups for a coffee refill at the hand of Elly.

"You might be right. I heard a rumor that Chivington's enlistment was up, but he hasn't said anything about leaving, and he's still recruiting more men for the 3rd Regiment, supposedly to protect Denver City. As you probably know, Reuben, the army is led by many men that have no business in leadership positions and are only there by political appointment," stated Wynkoop.

"Yup, we had more'n our share of political officers, none of 'em worth the powder to blow their nose!" replied Reuben, memories of his time in the Sharpshooters flashing through his mind.

"So, what's his latest plan concerning the Indians?" asked Bent, looking at the frustrated major.

"After he demanded Black Kettle order all the Dog Soldiers to surrender and come into the fort, and that didn't happen, he didn't want to listen when I told him that's not the way things work among the Cheyenne, but just because Black Kettle was the chief, Anthony thought he could order them to surrender, and they would." He shook his head and continued, "At the last parley we had with Black Kettle, Left Hand, and Little Raven, Anthony said he would continue our agreement, but he also said he was under orders not to provide the native people with any more rations. He went on to say if they would give up their weapons and move their people away from the fort, preferably to Sand Creek, that he would honor my promise of protection." Wynkoop paused, huffed a little and added, "When Black Kettle said he was concerned other soldiers wouldn't honor the agreement, Anthony just told him to wave the American Flag over his lodge and he'd be alright."

Wynkoop took a deep breath that lifted his shoulders, exhaled, "I assured Black Kettle it'd be alright and that I was only leaving to confer with the big chief over the army. But Black Kettle and Left Hand said they'd move their people."

"What about Little Raven?" asked Reuben, thinking of his friend and his Arapaho people.

"He didn't say anything, but 'fore I left the fort, I saw his people packin' up just like the others." Major Wynkoop sipped his coffee again, looked from Bent to Reuben, "It's just that we keep getting reports of the Dogmen and Sioux still attacking troops in Nebraska and Kansas territory, thankfully there have not been any recently in our country, but there's no tellin' about them."

"So, you're leavin' in the mornin'?" asked Bent, looking to Wynkoop.

"Ummhmmm, can't do anything more here, maybe Curtis will listen." Wynkoop stood, tossed the dregs of the coffee off the porch, and set the cup on the little table. He extended his hand and Bent and Reuben stood to shake with the man.

"You're gonna be missed around here, Major," offered Bent as he shook the man's hand and slapped his shoulder. "You've done well, and here's hopin' it'll help."

"I certainly hope so, Bill, I hope so," he answered, and turned to Reuben to shake his hand.

"Major, we'll be prayin' for you and trustin' you'll have a good assignment after this," suggested Reuben, as the men shook hands.

The major took the steps two at a time, snatched up the reins from the hitchrail and swung aboard his mount. With a touch to the brim of his hat, he nodded, turned away and rode out of the stockade. Bent and Reuben looked at one another just as Elly came from within, holding the hot pot of coffee with a pair of potholders and with a nod, offered the men a refill. Both gladly accepted and returned to their seats, Reuben nodded to Elly to suggest she join them, and she set the coffee pot on the end of the bench and sat beside Reuben. She asked, "You two are looking a little glum, bad news?"

Reuben frowned, thinking, "Not necessarily, just not good news. Things are changing for the natives; most of 'em are moving away from the fort, goin' to Sand Creek."

"Little Raven too?"

"Dunno. He's a little too cagey to be goin' with the others. I'm thinkin' he'll probably go somewhere else by themselves." He glanced to Bent, "What do you think, Bill?"

"You're prob'ly right, although you know him better'n I do, but I am kinda surprised that Black Kettle and Left Hand were so easily persuaded to go back to Sand Creek."

"Well, we were there, it's not a bad area. Good graze, good water, the rolling hills give some protection from the weather."

"But it's wide open, no protection from attack," mused Bent, frowning and sipping at the hot coffee.

Reuben frowned, "You don't think..." he began, but looked at Bent to answer.

"I don't think any of these soldier boys can be trusted, now that Wynkoop is gone."

Reuben looked at Elly, back at Bent, "I think maybe we'll go visit with Little Raven, maybe tomorrow or the day after, once he's got his camp settled in, wherever that may be."

———

"GENERAL CONNOR, I HAVE NO AUTHORITY TO ORDER Colonel Chivington to give you any troops!" exclaimed Governor Evans, looking at the uniformed general before him.

"I thought the 3rd Regiment was raised to provide protection for Denver under your orders!" exclaimed the General. He had come to procure the Colorado 3rd Regiment to gain strength to fight the Dogmen and Sioux in the northern routes.

"Even if I had the authority, I would not let them leave, they are for the protection of the citizens of Denver City!" proclaimed the governor. He glanced at Colonel Chivington who was visibly fuming, his neck and face turning red with anger.

"Your problem is not the number of troops! You can't find the Indians to fight 'em!" growled Chivington, "Now Colonel Shoup and I are the only ones that can find the blasted redskins!" He pursed his lips, the jaw muscles flexing, as he turned away, clenching his fists at his sides. General Connor glared at his subordinate and the governor, turned on his heel and stomped out of the office, slamming the door behind him.

The governor looked at Chivington, "Tell me you've got something going! Because if that upstart from Utah makes a successful strike against the Indians, our political aspirations will die with them!"

Chivington shook his head, still too angered to be seated and paced around the office as he began to explain, "I've got troops already on the move, but for your own protection, you don't need to know the rest. You'll get word soon enough." He turned and walked from the office, joined just outside the office door by his subordinate, Captain Joseph Maynard. Chivington glared at the man, "Report!"

"Sir! We received word that the seven companies of the Colorado 3rd and three Denver companies of the 1st regiment are enroute to Camp Fillmore on the Arkansas. As ordered, Colonel Shoup retrieved the remainder of the 100-day enlistees and they are marching toward the Arkansas!"

"Does anyone else know of these movements?"

"No one, sir!"

Chivington stopped and looked at the captain, "You mean, no one that you know of, don't you Captain?"

"Uh, yessir, Colonel, Sir."

The two men kept up their quick pace as they marched toward the livery to fetch their horses. It had already been planned that they would hasten far to the south to join the 3rd, preferably before the regiment reached Camp Fillmore on the Arkansas.

31 / RIDE

They rode into the sunrise, enjoying the cool of the morning, the chuckling waters of the Arkansas River their constant companion. Bear was out front and would often disappear into the brush or sage or over the next rise, but when he came back, Reuben knew he had spotted something that deserved attention. He reined up, leaned down to look at the dog, "What is it boy?'

Bear looked up at Reuben, mouth open and tail wagging, which told Reuben it was not imminent danger, but something worth looking at so he told Elly, "Stay ready, if you need cover," nodding to the trees at the riverside, "take to the cottonwoods."

Elly nodded, slipping her Henry from the scabbard and lay it across the pommel. She leaned forward to stroke the neck of the appaloosa, "Easy girl, we'll just wait here a spell."

With a quick nod, Reuben motioned for Bear to lead the way and the big blue roan followed at a trot. The wagon road that followed the south side of the river crested a slight rise and the big dog disappeared over the top. Reuben slowed Blue with a taut rein, slipped his

Henry from the scabbard, and lay it across the pommel and nudged his mount forward. He stood in his stirrups to get a look see before totally exposing himself and saw the first wagons of a slow-moving line of freighters pulled by triple yokes of oxen. Bull whackers walked alongside the big beasts, keeping them moving with whips, shouts, and even poking the animals with the butts of the whips. One man was mounted on a bay horse and leading the way, but as Reuben watched the man grabbed his rifle and lifted it to take aim at Bear. The big dog had stopped beside the road, head down and watching the approaching wagons. Reuben slapped legs to Blue and shouted, "Hold on there!" to stop the shooter. The man lifted his rifle just as he fired and the bullet went whistling away.

Reuben shook his head and rode up to the mounted man, "That's my dog you were getting ready to shoot! You just shoot at anything that walks?" growled an angry Reuben.

"I thought it was a big timber wolf!" retorted the man, slipping his rifle back in the scabbard. "How was I s'posed to know he was yore dog, he's big 'nuff to be a wolf!"

"The only wolves around this country are scraggly desert wolves, and I ain't seen a black one, ever!" replied Reuben. He took a deep breath, turned to look at the freighters, and back to the would-be shooter, "Where you headed?"

"Gold fields, if it's any of your business!" retorted the scruffy looking man who sat scowling at Reuben.

"Just thought I'd give you a fair warning about the Indians in this country."

"Injuns? What Injuns? We ain't seen no heathen redskins! But if we do, we'll give 'em what fer!"

Reuben stood in his stirrups to look back along the wagons, counted six, each with a triple yoke of oxen and each with one bullwhacker walking alongside. He dropped into his seat, looked at the rider, "You the ramrod of this outfit?"

"That's right. My name's Jackson Foster and I'm the owner and head teamster."

"Well, Mr. Foster, have you brought freighters out to this country before?" asked Reuben.

"This is our first trip, but it won't be our last! Mind you, there's a lot of people that need the supplies we can bring. We heard that Denver City was shut off and in desperate need of supplies. If we have any left after the gold fields, we'll go there. But we're prepared to make as many trips as necessary."

"So, you're familiar with the Indians wars that have been goin' on around here?"

The man frowned and squirmed in his saddle and lowered his voice as he asked, "Injun wars?"

"That right."

"No one said anything 'bout no Injun wars. Oh, some said we might run into some Injuns, but nothin' 'bout no Injun wars."

"You're lucky you haven't been hit already."

"Well, ever man has a Spencer repeater rifle and some o' the men were soldiers an' they know how to use 'em. We'll be alright," began Foster, looking around at the rolling countryside.

"So, you've got what, six men and yourself?" asked Reuben.

"No, by gum. We got six teamsters, and six roustabouts, an' me!" boasted the man, rearing his shoulders back in an attempt at bravado.

Reuben shook his head, "Most Indian war parties will

have fifteen to twenty experienced warriors, and some of them have captured Spencer rifles, but they can shoot six arrows in the time it takes a white man to pick a target and pull the trigger."

Foster leaned to the side and looked past Reuben, frowning. "That one o' your'n?" pointing to the rise of the knoll.

Reuben twisted around to see Elly coming toward them at a canter, the mule following close behind. She was waving and Reuben frowned, reining Blue around to face her, as he answered Foster, "Yeah, that's my wife!"

"Yore wife?"

Elly reined up beside Reuben, pointed toward the river, "War party, there!"

Reuben looked at Foster, "You best circle up your wagons as quick as you can, warn your men to get their rifles ready! But don't shoot until I give the word! They could be peaceful!"

Reuben looked to Elly, "Could you tell who they were?"

"No, but it looked like they had paint."

Reuben looked round about them, pointed to a point of rocks with some piñon, "There!"

Elly dug heels to her appy and motioned to Bear as they started for the rocky formation. Reuben looked at the freighters that had begun to pull into a formation with all the oxen in the middle, the back ends of the wagons forming a shape like the spokes of a wagon wheel. He shook his head but saw the men taking their positions in the back of the wagons, well protected by the thick wood tailgates. With a grin, Reuben moved closer to the wagon master and said, "I'm goin' into the trees, there, to have a closer look at the war party. Make sure your men don't go gettin' spooked and start shootin' at me!"

"I'll pass the word," replied Foster, and started around the circular formation, telling each of the men about Reuben.

Reuben kept well back in the trees but could see the band as they rode slowly along the north bank of the river. He saw several of the warriors with the scalplock at the back of their head, feathers fluttering, others with tall-standing roaches also with feathers. The long braids were wrapped with rabbit fur and hung over their chests. Several had hair pipe bone breast plates, and most had fringed leggings and beaded breechcloths. *They're Arapaho, alright.* Reuben shook his head as he watched, squinted at the sight of one of the leaders and recognized the younger Little Raven. He nudged Blue forward to break from the trees and called out, "HO! Little Raven!" He sat still, holding his right hand high, palm forward and open. "I am Man with the Blue Horse, a friend of your father, Little Raven." He nudged Blue forward, pushing into the river and starting across. The war party had stopped, most facing the white man, Little Raven coming to the front to watch the man cross the river. As Reuben came from the water, Little Raven asked gruffly, "Why are you here!"

"We're on our way to see your father, maybe spend a day or two with your people. My woman," he nodded behind him, "Yellow Bird, is anxious to see your mother, Red Bear and her friends, Running Antelope and Wind in her Hair."

Reuben paused, looking at the many warriors painted for war, and back to Little Raven, "We have much to talk to your father, much to say about the soldiers and the peace parley."

214

"There will be no peace!" spat Little Raven. "The blue coats want only to fight! We shall take their scalps!" he shouted, prompting many of the others to scream their war cries.

"Each must do as he believes is right, that is the way of your people. But we are friends of your father, Little Raven, and will always be friends."

Little Raven snarled, and asked, "The wagons, there, are they yours?"

"No, but they are friends of mine. They mean you no harm and wish to pass without a fight."

"We will kill them and take their goods! They have rifles, we want those rifles!"

"You will lose many warriors. Those men have fast shooting rifles, and one man can shoot like five men! Is it worth the lives of most of your men so a few may have rifles? And would you fight the friends of your father's friends?"

The warriors behind them had become silent, listening as the two men spoke in the tongue of the Arapaho. When rifles were mentioned, the warriors stirred, mumbling, and even shouting. But when he said most would die, and the rifles were not worth the death of even one warrior, they became silent. When Reuben spoke of friends, the warriors looked to one another and to Little Raven who was visibly upset, but also concerned about going against the friend of his father. He glared at Reuben, "Because you are the friend of my father who is also the chief of my people, I will not go against you and your friends. But if they are not your friends, they will die!"

"Your scouts can see these men protect my woman, they are my friends," answered Reuben, reining Blue around to give his back to the warriors and return across

215

the river. When he came from the water, he looked back, and the warriors were gone. He shook his head and drew a deep breath of relief, and nudged Blue from the trees to return to the wagons.

As he came to the wagons, Elly pushed out from the midst and came to his side. Reuben looked at Foster, "You are almighty lucky. I knew those warriors, they're Arapaho and their leader is the son of a friend of mine, Little Raven. That band has raided many ranches, taken other wagon trains, and killed many white men and taken captives. But because I said you were my friends, they left and will not attack. But if they get the idea I was lying to them, they'll take you and come after me. So, the best thing you can do, is make good time between here and Fort Lyon. You're less than twenty miles from the fort, and if you're smart, you won't stop until you get there!"

32 / SUSPICIONS

It was late afternoon when Reuben and Elly came in sight of the encampment they believed to be that of Little Raven and his people. The forty plus lodges were arrayed in a low swale between some low rising buttes, two small streams twisted their way through the village and families were busily preparing meals, children playing, and warriors crafting arrows and more. It was a new encampment and there was much to do to make it more habitable, although the people were accustomed to moving their camps often and with little or no forewarning. Reuben glanced to Elly and the two showed relief with faint smiles, concern still residing behind the expressions.

They started off the slight rise toward the camp as several mounted warriors came charging toward them but slowed when Reuben lifted his one hand and called out, "I am Man with the Blue Horse and this is my woman, Yellow Bird. We come to see our friends Little Raven and his woman." The warriors moved to the side, stoic expressions showing, but several recognized the visitors and the moment of tension passed. As they neared the camp, several called out greetings and children reached out to pet Bear as he moved close to them, eager for some attention and affection among these familiar people.

Little Raven flipped back the blanket that hung over the entry to his tipi and stepped out into the warm afternoon sun. A broad smile split his face when he saw Reuben and Elly. Red Bear followed her husband out and stood, shading her eyes as she looked to the visitors. When she recognized Elly, she smiled and walked quickly to her side to greet her. Elly leaned down, accepted Red Bear's hand, and slipped to the ground beside her friend. The women disappeared in a moment, Bear following on her heels, always protective. Reuben chuckled at his wife and her friends as he stepped down, handing the reins and lead to a young man summoned by Little Raven. The friends greeted one another with clasped hands and a shoulder bump, Raven motioning Reuben to the blanket and willow back rests. The men were seated as Raven said, "It is good to see my friend, and so soon."

"It is good to see you, Raven, and to know you and your people have chosen to make your camp away from those at Sand Creek where they were sent by the major at Fort Lyon."

Bear grinned, nodding, and looked at Reuben, his expression changing to stern, "I told you I do not trust the blue coats. Wynkoop gave his word, but the new major... there are lies in his words. He cannot be trusted."

"I agree my friend. That is why we came looking for you. I don't know what is happening, but..." shrugged Reuben. He shook his head and continued, "You and your people have long been our friends and I believe you have great wisdom. I know you have always talked peace, even though your son makes war, but your heart wants peace and I want peace also. But the blue coat Chivington and the governor have both said they want to destroy or kill all native people." He continued to shake his head, breathing deeply, and continued, "Not all white people feel that way, there are good among them, just like there are good and bad among the natives."

"Yes, I agree there are good and bad among all people. But until the good can show they will keep their word, treat my people with honor, we cannot trust them and must protect our people." Little Raven looked at Reuben, "You will stay with us?"

"For a few days, yes, if my friend will have us."

"You and Yellow Bird will always have a place with our people," answered Raven, nodding to the returning women, now with Running Antelope and Wind in her Hair, to prepare the lodge and the meal for their visitors.

———

"I'm tellin' ya Bill, there's somethin' amiss!" declared John Smith, looking at his friend William Bent as the two sat on the porch of Bent's home, overlooking the bosque of the confluence of the Purgatoire and Arkansas Rivers.

"What'chu mean, John?" queried Bent, frowning at his friend.

"Wal, the telegrapher at the fort done tol' me that Anthony reported to General Curtis that he agreed with Wynkoop's doin's with the natives to keep 'em quiet, but only 'till they had 'nuff troops for their offensive against 'em all!" He shook his head, sipped the steaming brew, and looked back at Bent, "An' thar' was a small-time trader come thru, we had a drink at the sutler's, an' he said he saw more soldiers than he thought was fightin' back east! Said they was ridin' an' marchin' south. He din't get close 'nuff to know what outfit they was or who the commander was, but he had heard things up by Russellville 'bout Chivington on the move."

"Chivington?!" spat Bent, "That parson colonel oughta be run outta the state! He's as worthless as teets on a boar hog!" Bent shook his head, fuming, "Him 'n that blasted governor wanna kill all the Indians an' then go to Washington an' brag about it! They don't give two hoots 'bout all the rest of us left behind and what'll happen when all the tribes get together!"

"What'chu think we oughta do?" asked Smith, leaning forward, elbows on his knees as he held the steaming coffee under his nose.

"Whar'd that fella say he saw the troops?"

"The way I recomember it, they was north of Fountain Creek, coming south along the hills thar."

"Camp Fillmore!" mumbled Bent, eyes going glassy as his mind began to churn.

"Huh?" asked Smith.

Bent looked at him, shook his head as he came back to the present, "I said, Camp Fillmore. That's where they're headin' and from there, follow the river east to Fort Lyon, yonder, and then go after the camps on Sand Creek!" He fumed as he considered the possibility, looked at Smith, "They need to be warned."

"Who? The natives?"

"Yeah, and two of my sons are with them!"

Smith considered, sipping his coffee. "Maybe I can do it, course we don't know fer shore anything like that's gonna happen! Do we?"

"No, but just in case, they should know."

"That agent, Colley, was talkin' 'bout takin' a load o' rations an' such to 'em at Sand Creek, thought I oughta' go with him."

"Then maybe you should. Mind you, I don't know for sure, but I think that might be what they're plannin' cuz I can't for the life of me, figger out any other reason for him to be movin' so many troops south. All the Dogmen and Sioux are attackin' in the north and east, it's been sorta peaceful down here."

Smith nodded, stood, and tossed the dregs of his coffee over the rail of the porch and set the cup down. He extended his hand to Bent, who stood to shake, and the men parted, each man with his own thoughts about what might be boiling just under the surface of the peaceful land.

———

THE LARGE ENCAMPMENT WAS LITTERED WITH DOG TENTS, shelters for the troopers that were made up of two shelter halves, buttoned together and using bayoneted rifles for uprights. The sun was lowering in the west when Colonel Chivington and his small entourage rode into Camp Fillmore on the Arkansas River. When he was spotted, the officers who had been together around the cookfire, jumped to their feet and went quickly to greet the Colonel. "Afternoon Colonel Chivington! We didn't expect you till sometime tomorrow!" declared a brash Lieutenant, snapping a salute that was copied by the others.

"That's obvious!" grumbled the Colonel, reluctantly returning the salute as he started to swing down. He looked over at Major Jacob Downing and Captain Joseph Maynard, "I want to see all officers at the fire, asap!" he growled. He dusted off his britches, removed his hat and slapped it against his thigh, dust flying every which way. He coughed, shook his head, and growled at a nearby Lieutenant, "Got'ny coffee?"

"Yessir, right away sir!" answered the young man, spinning on his heel to fetch the coffee.

When Chivington sat down on the camp stool, he leaned forward, elbows on knees, and stared at the flames. He heard the rustling of men coming near and he waited, without turning, for them to take their places. When the circle of officers stilled, he looked up as Major Downing said, "Everyone's here, sir."

Chivington leaned back, looked around the circle and slowly stood. He glared at each of the men and began, "We are going to strike a major blow against the renegade redskins that have been terrorizing this territory the last several months! I'll not give you all the details at this time, but you must make certain your men are able and willing to accomplish this monumental and historical task before us, failure will not even be considered. The lives of the people of this great territory are at stake! There are those in power that are looking to this land for the next state of the union and our nation is depending on us! We've been subjected to the murderous depredations of the heathen renegades long enough and we *will* put a stop to it!"

Most of the officers mumbled their agreement, looking to one another around the fire. These men had been wanting to get into the action for some time, few had been a part of the battle of Glorieta Pass, but most had yet to see any action. The Colorado 3rd Regiment was being called the Bloodless Third, and the men were tired of the misnomer. When most enlisted, they hoped to get into the war back east, but the uprising of the

Indians had predicated their posting in the territory of Colorado. Now was their opportunity to do what they enlisted to do, fight!

"We'll leave at first light. We have a two- or three-day march ahead of us. No one is to say a word about this! We will leave men at every settlement, every ranch, every stage station, to make certain that no one rides ahead to warn those that we are after. Is that clear?"

"Yessir!" proclaimed the officers in unison.

"Then let's hit the sack. Daylight comes early!" replied the Colonel, looking at the men as they turned away to go to their shelters. Major Downing and Captain Maynard had already ordered a tent erected for the Colonel and the Major escorted their commander to his quarters. Chivington turned to Major Downing, "Send for Colonel Shoup. I want a full report from him!"

Major Downing replied, "Yes sir! Right away sir!" turned to the captain, nodded, and said, "This looks like it!" and started to the large encampment for Colonel Shoup. With the captain by his side, the captain grinned, and said, "I think you're right Jacob, this is it." It was obvious that both men were eagerly anticipating the coming fight, as were most of the other six hundred and fifty troopers.

33 / CHIVINGTON

Colonel Shoup scratched on the Colonel's tent, heard "Enter!" and pushed the flap aside and stepped in, saluted Colonel Chivington and was motioned to sit in the lone chair while Chivington sat on the edge of the cot. He looked at Shoup, "And... ?"

"Uh, yessir. We have ten companies of the 3rd Cavalry Regiment and four companies of the 1st Regiment. That's a total of 500 militiamen and 125 1st Regiment soldiers."

"Good, good. Do you believe any word has gotten out with the troop movement?"

"I don't believe so, sir. But we've moved a lot of troops over considerable country and passed many settlements and ranches, so it is possible that there has been some that saw the troops, but no one knows where we are bound," answered Shoup. Colonel Shoup was a hand-picked officer of Chivington, having first come to his attention when he brought the Reynolds gang to Denver. Although he did not report the gang had been captured by two marshals and turned over to him. Shoup had curried favor with the Colonel and the governor and was given an unprecedented promotion from Lieutenant to Colonel and given command of the 3rd Regiment.

"Well, we will be taking steps to make sure word does not get out about our advance. That will be under your command, understand? No one must know, and that includes the commander and troops at Fort Lyon! I believe many of the officers and men have become sympathetic to the Indians and would give warning if allowed!"

"I understand sir!" declared Shoup, standing to salute, turn on his heel and leave.

———

THEY BROKE CAMP BY THE DIM GREY LIGHT OF EARLY morning, and with nothing more than coffee sloshing in their stomachs, the entire command was on the move. It promised to be a three-day journey over less than easy terrain and many of the militiamen were marching alongside the soldiers of the 1st Regiment.

It was late afternoon on the third day when the regiment neared the confluence of the Purgatoire and Arkansas River. Shoup had dispatched a squad under command of Captain Maynard to go to Bent's home atop the rise just south of the confluence and take control of the stockade. When Maynard and his squad rode into the open gate of the stockade, it was not a surprise to Bent, he had been watching the approach of the regiment for a while. As the captain reined up in front of Bent's porch, Bent stood atop the steps and with his ever-present cup of coffee in hand, his son Robert at his side, as he greeted the squad, "Aft'noon, gents. And to what do I owe the pleasure of your comp'ny?"

The captain barked, "Mr. Bent, you, and everyone

here are under orders to remain in your home! No one is allowed to leave, and we will post guards to keep you here!" He looked at the younger man, "Are you the son of William Bent?"

"I am. My name is Robert," replied the young man.

"You will come with us! NOW!" demanded the captain.

"Now hold on there! Just who do you think you are ordering us around. We're not in your confounded army!" growled Bent, tossing his coffee aside and setting the cup on the rail.

"No sir, you are not. But you are under Martial Law by order of Colonel Chivington and you," nodding to Robert, "are hereby conscripted as a guide to our regiment! Get your gear, now!"

Robert looked to his father, who nodded and motioned the young man into the house to get his gear. He quickly returned, dropped his gear, and trotted to the stable to fetch his horse. He soon returned and loaded his bedroll and rifle, swung aboard, and looked to the captain. With a glance to his father, who nodded his goodbye, Robert followed the captain as the squad, minus two guards left behind, departed the stockade.

Colonel Chivington led the regiment as they rode up to the fort, stopped and ordered Major Downing, "I want you to post pickets all around this fort. No man is to be allowed to leave. The pickets are ordered to shoot any 1st Regiment that tries to leave the post!"

"Yessir!" responded the major, turning to pass the order to a subordinate and watched as the pickets were ordered to take their place.

As previously arranged, Chivington and the officers rode into the compound to be greeted by Major Anthony. A grinning Anthony vaulted down the steps from the command post and snapped a salute to the Colonel. "Colonel Chivington! It is good to see you, sir!"

Chivington returned his salute and stepped down from his mount, removed his gloves and shook hands with Major Anthony, "Major. You are to prepare one hundred twenty-five of your troops to join our regiment. They are to have a week's rations, as much ammo as you can allow, and be prepared to march in," he snapped open his pocket watch, looked back at Anthony, "four hours!"

"Yes sir, Colonel sir!" replied an eager Anthony, snapping another salute. He turned on his heel and passed the order to Captain Soule and turned back to Chivington, "Would you join me for a drink, sir?"

"Of course. But first, I need to refresh myself. Have your aid bring in a basin of water and more."

"Yessir!" answered Anthony, turning to order Lieutenant Cramer to do as bidden.

"Join me!" ordered Chivington as he walked into the commandant's office.

Colonel Chivington was coming from the ante room, wiping his face and hands with a towel and began explaining his plan to Major Anthony. "We will leave after dark, march to this Sand Creek where the Cheyenne and Arapaho are camped," he paused, looked up at Anthony, "They're still there, aren't they?"

"Yessir."

"We'll hit them at first light. I've got three 12 pounder Napoleons and we'll bombard the village with them. We have five hundred 3rd Regiment militiamen, and with your men, we'll have two hundred fifty 1st Regiment troopers. Last word I received said there were almost a thousand renegade Indians camped here that went to

Sand Creek. So, I think we should be able to take care of that many, don't you?"

Anthony grinned, "Yessir, certainly sir."

"Good, good. Now, where's that drink?" he asked, seating himself in the big chair behind the commandant's desk. Anthony went to a small cabinet, removed a bottle and some glasses, and began pouring. A sudden rapping at the door startled him, but he answered, "Enter!"

Captain Soule and Lieutenant Cramer, officers that had served with Major Wynkoop, led a contingent of officers into the commandant's office. All saluted the Colonel and waited for his return salute, which was slow in coming. Chivington frowned and asked, "What is this all about?"

Captain Soule looked at the other officers and with a slight nod from the group, began to explain, "Sir, we understand from the men that you intend to attack the village of the natives at Sand Creek, is this true?"

"I don't know what concern that is of yours other than you have to obey orders, but yes, that is true. We intend to strike a decisive blow against the renegade heathens once and for all. We're tired of their depredations and murder, and it must be stopped!" growled the Colonel, remaining seated although very agitated as he glared at the group of officers.

"We are here to protest," began Captain Soule, "Major Wynkoop, at *your* direction, struck a treaty with those natives, Black Kettle, Left Hand, and others. You told him to get them to surrender, and they did, and now they are camped peacefully, expecting what was promised. Colonel, Indian Agent Dexter Colley, interpreter John Smith, Private David Louderback, and a wagon driver, Watson Clark, are now camped with the

Cheyenne and distributing rations and trade goods. We cannot attack them, sir, they are at peace with us!"

Colonel Chivington jumped to his feet and leaned over the desk to shake his fist at the officers, "I am in command here! Don't you dare question my authority nor my commands! You will do as you are ordered! Is that clear!" barked the angry Colonel.

But Captain Soule was determined and responded, "Black Kettle's band and the others are clearly camped as prisoners under the protection of the U.S. Army just as Major Wynkoop's truce required!"

"Wynkoop is an idiot! He had no authority to make any truce! Nor did he have the authority to allow distribution of rations to those heathens!" shouted the Colonel, sweat drops beading on his forehead.

"You gave him that authority at the meeting in Denver City in the governor's office! I was there and heard it!" declared a defiant Soule. Lieutenant Cramer and the other junior officers stepped between Soule and Chivington, pushing the captain back and talking softly to him, trying to stop the argument. As they returned to some form of rank, the Colonel stood back, glaring at each of the men, he shook his finger at Soule and growled, "I will kill you or any other soldier that dares to disobey me! Damn any man in sympathy with the Indians!"

Major Anthony stepped before the desk and looked at the officers, "Now, go to your posts and await further orders! Now!" he demanded, motioning to the door. The contingent of officers turned and left, mumbling as they did. Colonel Chivington dropped into the chair, reached for the drink, and after sloshing it down, he glared at Anthony, "Those men best obey, if they know what's good for them. I will broker no malcontents or disobedience!"

"I understand sir. Those are good officers, and I am certain they will conduct themselves accordingly," encouraged Anthony.

"We'll see, we'll see," growled Chivington, holding out his glass for a refill.

34 / SAND CREEK

High overhead a bright sliver of moon hung in the lonesome sky, while in the east, one star shone as a beacon of hope stranded in the dim shadowy sea of the heavens. Dark shadows of long clouds scarred the grey blue of the early morning sky as whispered movements of horses and men rode the morning breeze across the grassy rolling prairie. Tipi poles scratched at the fading sky looking like inverted spiders clawing to be set aright. From the tall lodgepole of a central lodge, a banner of red, white, and blue fluttered in the quiet of the sleeping village.

The serene scene was suddenly shattered by the explosion of 12-pounder Napoleon cannons, squatting on the low hills to the north, west, and south. The blast of bugles and the shouts of soldiers began to build into a cacophony of terror as rifles roared and sabers whistled in death wielding arcs. Screams of women and children collided with war cries of warriors, thundering hooves of charging horses, curses of soldiers, and barked commands of officers. Pistols cracked, rifles blasted, arrows whispered, and death marched among the masses.

Within moments, the bowl that had harbored families and homes, began to fill with the blood of innocents. Screaming women snatched up younger children to flee from the fight, running to the dry creek bed, older children trying to follow. Some of the warriors grabbed what weapons they had, bows and arrows, lances, and war clubs, to fight back, but their weapons were no match for the cannons and rifles of the soldiers. Bullets whistled overhead, torches were thrown into the lodges, smoke from the fires braided with the smoke from rifles and cannon. One woman, stumbled and fell, lifting an arm to protect her face as a cavalryman struck with his saber, breaking her arm, and splitting it open. She turned, lifted the other and again the man struck with his saber, breaking her other arm. With both arms broken and bleeding the woman shook with her sobs, believing death was coming, but the cavalryman laughed, and rode away, leaving her to bleed to death. The thunderous roar of the cannon, grape shot whining through the air, and the screams and war cries did little to mask the death cries of so many women and children.

Warriors rallied around the women, guarding them with their bodies and their lives, but angry cavalry, bloodlust in their eyes, charged through the warriors, slicing them open with sabers, shooting them down with pistols, and running over the women, shod hooves smashing skulls. White Antelope, a chief that sought peace, stood before his lodge, waving a white flag, and screaming at the soldiers, only to be shot down and pinned to the ground with bayonets as he choked his last.

A gathering of soldiers sat their horses on the south

rise, watching. Captain Soule and Lieutenant Cramer, commanding Company D and Company K of the 1st Colorado Cavalry, had refused to obey Chivington's command and now sat watching the horrors of the intended massacre. Cramer moved beside Soule, "You know we will be court martialed for this!"

"I'd rather face a court martial for disobeying a tyrant than for murdering a people that sought only peace and were here for our protection. If there was any way possible, I would do something to protect them, but those," nodding toward the screaming melee, "are not soldiers, they're monsters!" As they spoke, they saw a cavalry officer chase after a fleeing woman, his saber raised and as he passed, he slashed down, almost decapitating the woman. Blood spurted as her body crumbled, and Soule leaned over to puke his guts out. Unashamed, he sat upright, wiped his face clean and looked at Cramer, "Watch, and remember, for we will be called to testify of this madness!"

Smoke lay in the bowl like a rising flood, the tipi poles protruding above the river of grey. Charging horses parted the thick fumes with only the head and shoulders of the riders showing, some shooting rifles, most with pistols and sabers. Crazed soldiers and militiamen ran from lodge to lodge, searching for victims, blood shot eyes blazing, the stench of alcohol reeking from their curses, as they sought targets and trophies. A small group of warriors, standing back-to-back, were firing their antiquated rifles and once emptied, grabbed the barrels to use the stocks as clubs while the others launched a barrage of arrows into the blue tide.

Many of the fleeing Cheyenne and few Arapaho took to the sandy draw, using the banks for cover, began to dig into the banks and sand, trying to hide from the maddened killers. One naked child of about three summers was trying to find his mother who had fled with an infant in arms, struggled in the sand, arms flailing in terror, was spotted by a horseback rifleman. The soldier reined up, dropped to the ground, and lifted his rifle, taking aim at the fleeing child less than seventy-five yards away. But his aim was off, and the bullet plowed sand beyond the boy. Another cavalryman saw his friend miss and reined up, dropped to the ground beside him, "Let me show you how to get them nits!" as he took aim, but he also missed. The men looked at one another laughing as they reloaded while a third man, dropped alongside them, and from his standing stance, took aim, fired, and dropped the child into the sandy creek bottom. The three men laughed, remounted, and went in search of another target.

Several militiamen, knowing this would be their last chance at glory, moved almost shoulder to shoulder through the camp, stepping between burning lodges and saw one woman, swollen with child, crawl from a lodge. One man shouted, "This'ns mine!" and charged forward, lifted his rifle, and viciously slammed the butt plate into the woman's skull. He laughed and watched as she fell face first into the dirt. When she moaned, he snatched his bayonet from the scabbard at his waist, used his foot to roll her to her back, and cut her belly open, and with the knife blade, dragged the infant from her belly, casting it aside. He stood, snarled, looking at his handiwork, "That'n won't kill no more white men!" and walked away.

His companions sought others, but there were no living targets nearby. One shouted, "Hey, we need some trophies! Let's cut 'em up!" and they each found a body and began mutilating them. Scalps were taken from each

234

one, woman, child, even infants, as well as white haired old people and the few downed warriors. Body parts were cut away to use as jewelry, making necklaces of fingers, noses, and ears. Two officers walked side by side, cutting off the ears of every body they found. Many had genitals and breasts removed as some were heard to say, "These'll make good tobacco pouches!" to the laughter of others. Even Chivington and his senior officers were seen taking trophies of scalps and body parts, that would later be displayed as they rode triumphantly into Denver City.

There were a few soldiers that lay among the dead, later to be found the product of crossfire from over eager militiamen, for most rifles had been confiscated from the natives. The cacophony of battle waned as the natives fled, some catching horses from the herd, others capturing horses from the cavalry, most fleeing on foot. They fled up the sandy draw and as they fled, cannon to the south found them to be easy targets. The artillery resounded with the thunderous roar and screaming whistles of cannonball that had already been so deadly and continued their murderous onslaught.

The officers gathered on a slight knoll with a cluster of juniper and piñon, stepped down and stood in the shade, the morning sun now blazing down on the carnage. Chivington looked at Major Downing and Captain Maynard, "You two, take a couple men with you and make a count. I want a count of the dead and wounded enemy, and of our own. I plan to send a dispatch to the governor within the hour!"

The two men mounted up, choosing two other mounted men, and started to the midst of the battle site. The cannons had been silenced, war cries no longer lifted, but moans and cries of the wounded and grieving

235

could be heard. As they moved about, Downing and his man counted the natives, Maynard and his man counted the soldiers. Whenever they encountered a wounded native, regardless of age or sex, they were dispatched with a pistol shot. As the men finished their count, which was more of an estimate than accurate count, they returned to Chivington to report. When they dropped to the ground to join the Colonel in the shade, Major Downing reported, "Over two hundred natives dead, closer to two hundred fifty, sir!" He paused but decided against explaining that most of the dead were women and children.

"Bah! There's more'n that! Did you count them in the creek bottom?" growled the bearded Chivington, his uniform straining at the buttons as he proudly pushed forth his middle.

"Yessir! But there are probably more further on," replied the major.

Chivington glared at Captain Maynard, "And?"

"First Cavalry reports four killed and twenty-one wounded. Third Cavalry reports twenty killed and thirty-one wounded."

"That many? Don't seem right. Them hostiles didn't have but a few rifles, how's that possible?" mused the Colonel.

"Uh, beg pardon sir, but I think much of that was the crossfire from the different troops. Most of those killed and wounded were from rifle fire, sir."

Chivington frowned, "That will not show in your report, you hear me!" growled the Colonel, knowing that such a report could be devastating to his record.

"Yessir!" replied a recalcitrant Captain Maynard.

"I've already sent a dispatch to Denver! I estimate

there were five to six hundred Indian warriors killed and the Cheyenne have been thoroughly routed!"

The other officers frowned, looking at one another, until Major Anthony asked, "Sir, should we ready the men to go after the Dog Soldiers and the Sioux as you said?"

"Hummph, no! We're going to hunt down Little Raven. Smith tells me his people were not here and he needs to be thoroughly whipped as well!" He shook his head as he glowered at the officers, "We leave in one hour! That'll give the men enough time to gather their trophies!" snickered the Colonel, turning to seat himself in the shade of the big juniper. He motioned to Major Downing, "Have someone fix us some coffee, I need some before we leave. It's been a tiring battle!" as he leaned back, stretched out and covered his face with his hat.

35 / AFTERMATH

Little Raven stood, Reuben at his side, watching the warriors follow his son, Little Raven, into the central circle of the village. The young war leader scowled, held his feathered coup stick high, scalps wafting in the breeze. "Ho, my chief, and my father!" he began, looking sternly at the respected leader of the Arapaho people. "I bring bad news. The blue coats, that you begged for peace, have brought death to the people of Black Kettle and Left Hand! War Bonnet, White Antelope, Lone Bear, Yellow Wolf, Big Man, Bear Man, Spotted Crow, Bear Robe, and Left Hand have crossed over! Their bodies mutilated by the blue coats! Women and children lie among the ashes of their lodges! *This* is the peace you want?"

The villagers had gathered around as the younger Little Raven led his warriors into the midst of the village and now crowded near, they began to wail at the story of so many that had crossed over. Chief Little Raven raised his arms high, looked from his son to the many people and elders of the *Hinono'eino.* "My son brings dark news of our friends and families. We will honor them as we mourn them." He looked at his son, "The blue coats?"

"Even now they search for your village, but they are far north and know not where to look," answered the younger Raven.

The chief looked at the people, raised his voice, "We will move our village, we will go south across the river into the land of the Kiowa." The people quickly responded, and the chief knew they would be on the move within the hour. He looked at his son, "You will watch the blue coats, lead them away from our people."

"And if we kill many?"

"Then honor those who have crossed over. I will go to the village of Black Kettle, see that of which you speak. I must honor the dead of our people," explained the chief, dismissing his son and his warriors with a wave of his hand. Little Raven lifted his coup stick, motioning to his warriors and as they started from the camp, several of those that had remained with the village had gathered their weapons and mounted their war ponies to join the younger Raven.

The chief turned to Reuben, "My woman, Red Bear, who is also our shaman, will go with me. Will you and Yellow Bird join us?"

"We will," replied Reuben, anxious to see the site of what the young warrior had spoken. If it was as he thought, it would be a scar on the face of history for years to come. Within moments, he and Elly, were mounted, their pack mule loaded, and were waiting for Little Raven and Red Bear.

The four rode in silence, watchful for any soldiers or other dangers and taking a circuitous route to the encampment site at Sand Creek. It was late afternoon; the sky was clouded and rumbles in the distance warned of a coming storm. They saw the signs of the many soldiers, tracks of the wagons and artillery, churned soil from so many horses, and cast offs that told of their passing. When they crested the low knoll that overlooked the bowl with the remains of the village, they stopped, moving side by side as they looked at the smoldering embers that spoke of destroyed lodges. Carrion eaters had already gathered and were now fighting and snarling as they fought one another for the remains of so many dead. Turkey buzzards floated on updrafts, many already tearing at the carcasses, others fighting off ravens and whiskey jacks. Coyotes trotted from body to body, grabbing bits of flesh as they moved. Badgers claimed dominion over several bodies, while lesser predators snarled and hissed at one another.

As they sat, looking at the desecration, a bolt of lightning exploded a lone juniper on the far side of the camp, jolting the observers from their trance. Big drops of rain began to pelt them, quickly soaking through their buckskin attire, yet Little Raven lifted both hands heavenward, his face tilted upwards as he began to chant a song of mourning. As he finished, he looked at the others, "Even the Great Spirit weeps for this! He washes away the evil and the blood with His tears!" He lowered his eyes, lifted the reins of his mount, and led the others to ride through the camp, looking at the destruction and carnage. Elly reined up, slid to the ground, and sloshed through the mud to the far side of a partially burned lodge and could be heard regurgitating. Reuben lost control of his innards and leaned forward to cast his puke aside, then lifted his face to the rain and let the water run down his face and neck.

Little Raven and Red Bear had continued on, leaving Reuben and Elly behind, but waited on the east side of the village. As they neared, Reuben looked at his friend and his woman, and explained, "We," nodding to Elly, "will leave here. You have been our friends and will always be our friends, but we cannot stay in a land that allows this," pointing back to the village with his chin. "We will return to our cabin in the valley of the Sangre de Cristo mountains, far to the west and south of here. Perhaps we will one day return to your land, or you may come to ours, but until then," he made a fist and put it over his heart, "you and your people will always be in our hearts!"

Little Raven nodded, glanced from Reuben to Elly and to his wife, Red Bear. The rain still came, hiding the tears that made salty rivers down their faces, but sadness was written on their faces. Little Raven pushed his mount alongside Reuben's roan, and the men clasped hands to bid their farewells. Elly and Red Bear did the same and the couples separated, turning once to look back at the other, and rode out of sight.

————

PREFERRING TO AVOID THE LAND OF THE COMANCHE, Reuben and Elly pointed their horses west. His plan was to pass north of Fort Pueblo and go to the small settlement of Cañon City. There they would resupply and turn south up Grape Creek to return to their cabin. They were four days on the trail when they saw the thin wisps of smoke this side of the long hog backs that told of the little settlement of Cañon City. The town had been founded to be supply point for the gold fields in South Park and had become a bit of a hub for stagecoach travel. As they rode into the little burg, Reuben spotted Morgan's Emporium and across the street was C.W.

Kitchen's General Store. They reined up in front of Kitchen's, stepped down and slapped reins over the hitchrail, tying off the lead for the pack mule. Elly said, "Think we can get somethin' to eat first? I'm hankerin' for a good meal that I don't hafta cook!" she giggled, smiling at Reuben.

Next to the general store was Ma's Café and they stepped inside, pausing to let their eyes adjust to the dim light. A table sat before the big window, three empty chairs showing in the shafts of light that harbored the many dust mites. Elly smiled, nodded, and they took the two chairs with their backs to the window and sat down. A matronly woman, probably the one who's name was on the sign, came to their table, wiping her hands on the frilled apron, "What can I fix ya?"

"What's the special?" asked Elly.

"We got No Name stew, an' we got some fried chicken left," she declared as she reached for the coffee pot that sat on the buffet over a candle. She poured the cups full as Elly looked at Reuben who said, "I'll take some chicken and a piece of that pie I see sittin' yonder!" grinning at the woman.

She chuckled and looked at Elly, "The same," said Elly, smiling.

As the woman left for the kitchen, they looked around the small café, saw one man sitting alone at a table in the corner, nodded to the stranger and looked to one another. As they turned, a soft voice came from the shadows, "You folks look like you've traveled a ways."

"Ummhmm, from the flats north of Fort Lyon," responded Reuben, frowning at the man. It was not a common thing for people to ask strangers where they've been or where they're going, but the man was not intimidating, appeared a little smaller than most and soft spoken, but he was attired in a buckskin jacket over blue uniform pants that bore the yellow stripe of cavalry.

"Up Sand Creek way?" asked the man, standing to come closer.

Reuben watched as the man came into the light. He had long blonde hair, small stature, standing about five and a half feet tall, but there was a confidence in his manner. He stood near and asked, "Hear anything about troopers down thataway?"

"What'chu want to know?" asked Reuben.

The man motioned to the extra chair, "Mind if I join you. I'm a little desperate for news."

Reuben nodded, watched as the man seated himself. The visitor held out his hand, "I'm Carson, most folks call me Kit."

Reuben frowned, glanced at Elly, and held his hand out to the man. "Reuben Grundy, and this is my wife, Elly."

"So, what can you tell me about the Indian situation there? I've heard rumors of things that don't sound too good, and I'm a mite concerned."

Reuben looked at the man, reached for his coffee, took a sip, and began to tell what they had seen. It took a while and as he spoke, the woman brought their food, and sat down to listen. Before he finished, there were three others that had drawn chairs near to hear. When he finished, he realized he had tears in his eyes and a lump in his throat and slowly shook his head as Elly reached out to grasp his hand. "No one should have to see what we saw," he finished.

No one spoke, each looking at the couple and then to one another until Carson said, "That dog Chivington and his filthy hounds, shootin' down squaws, murderin' little innocent children. Folks call such Christians, do ye?

And Indians savages? Whaddya s'pose our Heavenly Father, who made both of us, thinks of these things? I fought many a injun, but I ain't never drew a bead on a squaw or a papoose, and I despise the man that would!"

The small group added their agreement, shaking their heads in shame over what happened, but one man stormed out, mumbling something about *"Dirty redskins need to be kilt! All of 'em!"* but the disgust and contempt showed on the faces of those near the table of Reuben and Elly. The woman known as Ma, grabbed their plates and said, "Let me get you some hot food!" and went to the kitchen.

————

ELLY AND REUBEN RODE FROM CAÑON CITY WITH HEAVY hearts and heavy packs. Resupplied for the coming winter, they were hopeful of making it to their cabin before the snow came with a fury. There were patches of white in the trees, aspen were bare, with only a few stubbornly clinging to brown and yellow leaves. The air was chilly but fresh and when they broke from the trees, the wide panorama of the snow-capped Sangre de Cristo mountains welcomed them with timbered arms spread wide. They stopped to bask in the beauty, looked at one another and Elly said, "We're home!"

EPILOGUE

After Sand Creek –

ALTHOUGH CONDEMNED BY THE JOINT COMMITTEE ON the Conduct of the war, **Chivington** was never charged with wrongdoing. His enlistment had expired before he led the charge, yet he officially resigned the following February. He tried to run for political office but was labeled a "rotten, clerical hypocrite" by the *Omaha Daily Herald* and his career was ended. He later married his son's widow, and she divorced him for non-support. The remainder of his life was a dismal failure and string of bad debts. He died of cancer in 1894.

Chief Black Kettle continued to strive for peace, signing two more treaties, but stated, "It is hard for me to believe white men anymore." Four years after Sand Creek, Lt. George Custer led the 7th Cavalry to attack the Cheyenne village at Washita River in western Oklahoma. They killed more than 100 Natives. While trying to cross the river, Black Kettle and his wife were shot in the back and killed.

Chief Little Raven continued to seek peace for his people, signing two more treaties with the whites, both of which were broken by the whites. H stayed on the land of his reservation until forced off, and although he led his people to remain neutral during the *Red River War of 1874-75,* he eventually settled at Cantonment in Oklahoma and died in 1889.

William Bent returned to his ranch on the Purgatoire with his new wife, Adaline Harvey, but on a return trip to Missouri for supplies, he contracted pneumonia and died in 1869. His wife gave birth to their daughter and lived out her life in Colorado and died in 1905 at Pueblo Women's Hospital

Chief Left Hand, or Niwot, thought to have died at Sand Creek, went with some of his people to the reservation in Oklahoma where a 1907 *Baptist Home Monthly* (Vol.29, p.113) reported that "old Chief Left Hand" and 100 of his Arapahos had converted that January to the Baptist faith, quoting him as reminiscing about his more warlike days.

TAKE A LOOK: STONECROFT SAGA VOLUME ONE

BEST-SELLING AUTHOR B.N. RUNDELL TAKES YOU ON AN EPIC JOURNEY THROUGH THE OLD WEST IN THIS ACTION-PACKED 5-BOOK WESTERN COLLECTION.

After a bloody duel leaves one man dead, Gabriel Stonecroft along with his life-long friend, Ezra, are determined to leave town. A journey to the far wilderness of the west would soon begin.

One man from prominent social standing, the other with a life of practical experience, are soon joined in life building adventures.

"A fun fast paced book. Perfect for the outdoors history loving reader." – **John Theo Jr., author of the Brandon Hall Mysteries.**

Danger, excitement and never-ending adventure will follow the two friends as they face bounty hunters, river pirates and renegade Indians. With every turn they meet a new hurdle and just when they think they're on their way into the uncharted wilderness, they are faced with a new challenge, the like of which they never imagined.

Stonecroft Saga Volume One includes: Escape to Exile, Discovery of Destiny, Westward the Wilderness, Moonlight and Mountains and Raiders of the Rockies.

AVAILABLE NOW

ABOUT THE AUTHOR

Born and raised in Colorado into a family of ranchers and cowboys, **B.N. Rundell** is the youngest of seven sons. Juggling bull riding, skiing, and high school, graduation was a launching pad for a hitch in the Army Paratroopers. After the army, he finished his college education in Springfield, MO, and together with his wife and growing family, entered the ministry as a Baptist preacher.

Together, B.N. and Dawn raised four girls that are now married and have made them proud grandparents. With many years as a successful pastor and educator, he retired from the ministry and followed in the footsteps of his entrepreneurial father and started a successful insurance agency, which is now in the hands of his trusted nephew. He has also been a successful audiobook narrator and has recorded many books for several award-winning authors. Now finally realizing his life-long dream, B.N. has turned his efforts to writing a variety of books, from children's picture books and young adult adventure books, to the historical fiction and western genres which are his first love.